DATE NIGHT

SIX EROTIC SHORT STORIES

MIRIAM F. MARTIN

HERMIT MUSE PUBLISHING

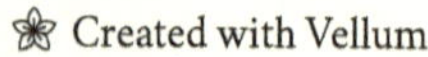 Created with Vellum

CONTENTS

THE LIFE OF CANDY

SOMETHING SWEET

"That's the story of my life," she said. It wasn't entirely true, but tonight, in this restaurant, with this man, it certainly felt true enough.

Candice sipped at the Pinot Noir served in a chipped plastic wine glass. She would've preferred a Merlot, but the waiter—a short, good natured but completely oblivious man who clearly only worked here for college money—insisted they no longer had anything but Pinot, and one that tasted like bitter sugar water.

So she leaned back in the squeaky wood chair. The cushion was flat from a thousand asses sitting in it, and the armrests felt sticky. She dared not look under the table, for fear of whatever it was she'd kicked around throughout the date.

The lighting was low, presumably for atmosphere, or mood, or some such thing. But in reality, it was probably to make the salmon pink wallpaper less repulsive.

Two different sets of music competed with each other. Light modern pop playing from the loud speaker directly above their table. And the heavy thump-thump-thump of a cover band playing in the sports bar next door. They were trying their best on "Heart Shaped Box," and sounded more like a hornets' nest amplified a thousand-fold.

Presumably, Abby's was a nice restaurant, at least according to people who maybe hadn't actually eaten there in the last decade or so. The tilapia tasted oddly like cod, and the baked potatoes were shriveled little bastards. The only good part of the meal was the breadsticks, which were buttery and garlicky, and practically melted in Candy's mouth. Thankfully, the waiter dude kept bringing those out in large baskets, six sticks at a time. Candy caught the guy eating a few himself, while he thought nobody was looking.

The other good thing about this date was Brad, the man sitting across from her. This was date number three, and he was still acting like a perfect gentleman. Opening doors for her, touching her gently on the elbow while riding the escalators in the mall, and he paid for the entire dates.

Also, he still hadn't made any moves, beyond sweet good night kisses and hugs. Candy worried that he was secretly gay, or hiding something. Like psychotic tendencies. Or a small penis.

But that was crazy thinking. He was just a nice guy, who wasn't in a rush to lift her skirt.

Even though she wore the shortest skirt she owned. The tight stretchy black one, with the slit that revealed one well muscled thigh. She wore six inch strappy black heels, which made her legs feel even longer, and made her the same height as Brad. Her gauzy purple blouse revealed more cleavage than she was used to revealing. And with a little help from her bra, her boobs seemed bigger than they had a right to be.

Brad was the tall, dark, and handsome type, in that order. His hair was long enough to be curly in the back. A permanent five o'clock shadow covered his face, which tickled Candy every time he kissed her.

He wore jeans and a black polo shirt, with shiny black dress shoes. Always relaxed, leaning back in his chair, as if his body were made for his clothes, and not the other way around.

He'd given up drinking the Pinot.

But he laughed at all of Candy's lame jokes, and made more than a few gut ripping punch lines himself.

"Come on, now," he said. "That's can't be entirely true. Can it?"

"It is," Candy said. "That really is the story of my life."

And then they both laughed, and reached for the same breadstick at the same time, which caused even more laughter.

She couldn't even properly remember what brought on this exact conversation. What the fuck was the story of her life? Ending up on good dates in bad places? Having fun where shouldn't be any fun?

All three of her dates with Brad should've been disasters. The first one was just a normal dinner and a movie date. But the restaurant he'd made reservations for just got closed down that afternoon after a health inspection, and then the movie theater was so full that they waited two hours and were turned away when the tickets were sold out. Instead, Brad and Candy walked along the waterfront, holding hands and throwing pennies into the river.

The second date was supposed to be bowling night, but they had the bad luck of going during the senior citizens' league night. Every old geezer hit on Candy, including some of the older women.

And then dinner at Abby's.

Earlier in the week Candy had decided, almost subconsciously, to make a contingency plan, just in case Brad chickened out. The plan involved a bag of Skittles, a TV marathon to catch up on the current crime dramas, and a fresh bottle of lube for her vibrator.

Luckily, Brad didn't chicken out.

He was a good sport. He pushed the breadstick basket over to her. Candy split the stick in half, took one half, and shoved the other back towards him.

Then they clinked plastic wine glasses in toast.

"Almost hate to ask what you want to do next," said Brad. "You know, given how your life story seems to be."

"Hey, now," Candy said. "It's not all bad. Mostly the bad stuff happens when I go out."

"Really? I've had a wonderful time."

"Kiss ass." Candy chewed on some breadstick. It wasn't as good as it was earlier. Less hot, not as garlicky. Brad seemed to agree, he put his down after one bite.

"So," he said. "If the bad luck only happens when you go out, maybe we should stay in?"

Now that was an idea. Candy had thought of that several times during the week leading up to her hot date. Well, to be honest, she mostly thought about that while using her vibrator. Which was why she needed a new bottle of lube.

Candy winked. "Your place or mine?"

Brad scratched the stubble on his chin and raised one eyebrow, which made her laugh. "My place has room mates," he said. "And they have girlfriends who might be having the same idea."

"Which idea is that?"

"The idea you're having, of course." He winked.

And then, Candy let the silence turn awkward. She let it hang there for a moment longer than necessary. Brad squirmed. He shifted in his chair, and looked down at his half eaten breadstick.

Candy burst out laughing. She winked at him. The hard

edge—that oops, what-did-I-do-wrong look in his face—softened, and he laughed too.

"My place," Candy said at last. For good measure, she picked up the breadstick and kissed the tip softly. "Unless you're not having the same idea."

He squirmed again, this time in a more playful way. As if he were adjusting his equipment inside his pants. "I'm having some wonderful ideas," he said.

"Good," she said.

Brad got his wallet out. She reached across the table and smacked his hand.

"I'm paying this time," Candy said. "You go to my place, you play by my rules."

"Okay," said Brad. "Any other rules I should know about?"

Candy smiled. She got out her credit card and tapped it on the table. "Nobody gets hurt. Ask permission for anything weird. Listen to instruction. Think you can handle that?"

He placed a hand on his chest. "I can do that."

"Good." Candy handed the card to the waiter dude. "By the way, the rules are more like guidelines. But the listening thing is rather important."

"As long as it goes both ways," he said.

"Yes!" she said. "But really. My vibrator is an excellent listener. Just so you know how you're being judged."

"Duly noted."

She paid. Then they left hand in hand. Candy couldn't keep her eyes off him.

Then, at her car, he kissed her. She gave him her address and promised to meet him there.

The drive home was far too long. She could barely drive straight, her hands shook so hard.

SOMETHING NAUGHTY

She didn't even make it home.

Brad texted her along the way. "Need condoms," he wrote. She noticed him pull into a convenience store at the corner. She turned around and parked her car next to his.

He seemed pleasantly surprised when he noticed her walk through the door.

"Not a lot of selection," he said, shaking his head. "Hope ribbed is okay with you."

"Fine by me," she leaned against him, and kissed him. The tip of her left breast poked at his arm.

Brad turned a little, rubbing her nipple with his arm very slowly. Then he casually flicked a finger across her breast. Just a light touch, as if he didn't even do it at all.

"How much further to your place?" he said. "I don't know if I can stand the wait much longer."

"Well don't explode before we get there," she said. "I'd hate to clean up after you here."

An elderly couple appeared at the end of the aisle. The old man shook his head and walked the other way. The old woman winked knowingly and chased off after her husband.

"Think that was a tad obvious?" Brad whispered.

Candy pressed her thumb and forefinger together. She whispered back, "Just a tad."

They both laughed. This really was Candy's luck. But at least it wasn't all bad luck. Strange luck, more like it.

An idea popped into her brain. She suddenly wanted to test her luck. Good or bad, this was going to be fun. She grabbed Brad by the arm and led him to the back of the store, to the women's bathroom.

"Wait," Brad said. She didn't wait. He turned a cute shade of pink around his ears. "Where are we going?"

She didn't give him the benefit of an answer. She peeped a quick glance over her shoulder and stepped inside.

"Hello," she said. When nobody responded, Candy dragged Brad inside. And then she pushed him inside the handicap stall and locked the door behind her.

"Can't say I saw this coming," he said.

She squatted down on her haunches in front of him. "Do you approve?"

"No," he said.

"Oh. Sorry." Well, that was disappointing. She stood up, trying not to let the disappointment show too obviously on her face. Her luck certainly ran out this time.

She turned to unlock the stall door. But he grabbed her by the elbow and turned her around.

"I didn't say I completely disapprove," he said. "I just don't completely approve of you going down on me here."

"We can finish this at my place," she said. "If you're still interested, of course."

And then he squatted down in front of her, hands on her pelvis. "Oh, we'll finish at your place. But while we're in the ladies' room, it will be ladies first."

"Oh," she said. "Oh, my."

He lifted her skirt up and pulled her panties down in two

swift motions. The air in the bathroom was a bit colder than she expected. Didn't help that her pussy was clean shaved. Usually she let it grow out, and maybe trimmed it now and then to keep the stink down.

But before the date tonight, Candy had been feeling frisky. She was now glad she spent the time to shave herself.

He rubbed his fingers across her bare thighs. And then closer to her pussy. Two fingers on her lips, and spread her apart for a moment. The motion was mechanical, not quite what she wanted, but he was attentive to her reactions.

"Too soon for this?" he said.

She shrugged one shoulder. "I want it. But yeah, this idea might've fizzled."

"How can we unfizzle it?" he said. "Is that even a word?"

Candy snorted. "Sure. It is now."

She rubbed her clit with one finger, slowly, as if she were masturbating at home. Still wasn't doing anything for her. Not yet. Usually a porno and a toy would do the trick. When she was by herself. But she certainly wasn't this time.

Brad kissed her thigh, and then stood up. Hands around her waist, he pulled her in for a kiss on the lips. A slow, sensual kiss, with slow tongue movement. He pressed her against the stall door, making the walls rattle. He tugged at her blouse, as if wanting to expose her breasts. She wanted him to. Hoped he would. He even found her bra strap, and tugged it down.

Then he kissed her shoulder, and set the bra strap back where it belonged. That little act of denial made Candy's skin tingle with heat. She flicked her clit faster.

Brad skimmed his lips down her chest, and lingered between her cleavage. His warm breath against her skin felt good. Felt right, as if his head were made to lay between her breasts like.

He squeezed each one, and then licked them both. So very

close to her nipples. If he just pulled down her blouse and her bra, he would've had them in his mouth. Instead, he inhaled her, and then got down between her legs again. He carefully stuck his tongue out and tasted her pussy.

She was surprised how wonderful that small touch felt. Not earth shaking, by any means. But sweet. Tender.

Then he pressed his mouth onto her pussy and licked her from clit to just below the anus.

Candy pressed her hands on both sides of her face. The bathroom started to smell musky, like wet pussy. He kept massaging her with his tongue, as if licking ice cream. By now he should've had a brain freeze. She imagined how light headed he must feel. He gripped both of her thighs to steady himself.

And then, while he massaged her clit with his tongue, he slipped the tip of one finger inside her. The way he slowly ate her drove Candy crazy. Now she couldn't wait to get to her place, for fear of exploding in the middle of a public place. Instead of cleaning up after him, he'd be cleaning up after her.

And when he slipped more than the tip of his finger in, she almost lost it.

Candy clamped a hand over her mouth. The scream was there, just below the surface, not quite ready to come out. But she wanted to scream.

She imagined a whole lot of people rushing into the bathroom, rushing to aid a screaming woman. And turns out she was screaming in orgasm.

She snorted back a laugh.

Brad pulled away. Her pussy felt cold without his tongue or finger inside her.

"You okay?" he asked.

"Yeah," she said. She cupped the back of his head and gently forced him back down on her.

He obliged willingly. He continued nibbling at her and fingering her, but more carefully this time, as if she were fragile. She leaned her head against the wall, wishing he'd do what he'd been doing before her snort.

Absent mindedly, Candy pressed a finger against her clit and rubbed while he finger fucked her. She closed her eyes, half aware of what she was doing. Yeah, it wasn't his doing, but it felt good.

And then he hit her G-spot, right on, and curled his finger against it. Her toes curled and she suppressed another scream.

And then she rubbed herself in the just right way. His finger inside her and her own finger doing some well practiced magic on herself, that combination sent her over the edge.

Her knees buckled, and if he hadn't been holding her legs upright, she'd have fallen over.

Once she regained her balance, Brad stood up and held her for a moment.

"There's a lot more I'd like to try with you," he said, and then kissed her on the mouth. He smelled of her. Kind of a sweet, musty smell. That odor probably wasn't leaving the bathroom for awhile.

"Oh? Is that so, mister?" she winked at him. And then she pushed him away. "Perhaps we find some place more cozy for what you have in mind?"

"Like your place? Like we meant to do."

"Sounds wonderful."

He helped her pull her panties back up, his fingers not quite helping, and ended up bunching her panties in a wad that rode her pussy lips. She straightened her skirt. Not like it mattered. With any more luck, she'd be out of these clothes soon anyway.

That was the plan for sure.

SOMETHING UNEXPECTED

*S*he was home at least, but that plan still hadn't come to fruition.

Sure, Brad had Candy pressed up against the wall, kissing her, both hands squeezing her boobs. She slid her fingers down his waist and tugged on his belt. Then tugged on something else just below the belt.

But the part of the plan about being out of her crooked clothing was coming about too slowly for her tastes.

She even said so, rather sloppily around kissing.

"Huh?" said Brad.

"Let's find somewhere more comfortable," she said.

He eagerly agreed and followed her upstairs to the bedroom. She'd left the bed-side light on earlier, which cast a yellow glow. She tossed her purse on the TV stand, next to the bag of Skittles, her contingency plan that thankfully she didn't need anymore.

"Taste the rainbow," Brad picked up the candy bag.

"Knock yourself out," Candy said. "Though I'd hope you'd make a better decision by this point in the night."

"Let's see," he said. "Which candy do I really want? Real conundrum here."

"Hey now!" She slapped him on the arm and moved to the bed to pull the sheets down. She was impressed he was able to use the word conundrum. Especially after being as worked up as he was.

She started to kick off her high heels, and thought otherwise. When was the last time she wore heels to bed? Sounded like a fun idea. She sat her ass on the side of the bed, and waited for Brad to decide on how to solve his conundrum.

He opened the box of condoms, and tossed one to the bed. Then he opened the candy and brought himself to bed.

"Having a little of both?" Candy said.

"Why the fuck not?" he said, and winked. He tossed a candy into his mouth.

And then he unzipped her skirt and pulled it and her panties to the floor. She took off her blouse, but left her bra on. She wanted him to decide on that one.

She helped him out of his polo shirt and jeans. He kicked his shoes to the side, and had the decency to take off his socks.

Clearly he worked out at the gym. Not big muscles, but he was well chiseled and formed. And the bulge in his boxers looked well formed too.

He pushed her down onto the mattress.

Before he could do anything else, she flipped over on her stomach.

"I think I owe you," she said.

"Is that so?" He didn't waste any time slipping off his boxers and getting in front of her face. He was long, much longer than she would've normally preferred. But she wasn't telling him that. Plus he was thick, which mattered more to her. He was cleanly shaved, except for a little patch of dark hair above the shaft.

Candy tugged on his balls, and then stroked his member. He waited patiently, on his knees in front of her, arms behind his back, not forcing himself, letting her take the lead.

She gripped him by the girth, and tugged him closer. He scooted an inch. Close enough for her to taste his tip and scratch her fingernails down his shaft. She took him in a little bit at a time. His breathing became panting.

He stroked her hair back and she swallowed him deeper yet. Not balls deep. She didn't have that kind of talent.

And thankfully, he didn't force her to deepthroat. Likely she would've gagged. And that just wasn't sexy.

And then he shifted a little to the side, and she heard the rustle of plastic. She spat him out and looked up. He popped a Skittle into his mouth.

"Want one?" he said, and offered her the bag.

She burst out laughing. Even spat a little on his cock on accident. "Seriously, dude?"

"I take all my pleasures seriously," he said, a wry grin on his sexy lips.

She took a candy and ate it, trying to chew it slowly. The effect wasn't as seductive as she hoped, and she burst out laughing again.

He laughed with her.

"Sorry," she said, when she finally settled down a little.

He shrugged. "What for? I'm having a wonderful time."

"Good," she said, and grabbed hold of his cock to bring him back to her.

The after-taste of the candy made him taste sugary. She thought about lines in bad erotica novels, about cocks that taste sweet like sugar or strawberries, and she suppressed another laugh. Brad responded with a guarded chuckle of his own, as if he wasn't sure what to think of her latest outburst.

And then she finally got serious about sucking his cock.

She couldn't fit him inside her mouth, so instead she

licked him down the shaft. First one way, then the other way back up. She wrapped her lips around his head, and flicked him with her tongue. And then back down again, leaving a sloppy mess to his sack. She sucked in one ball, then the other.

A soft moan from him told her to keep doing just that. She massaged his balls with her tongue while tugging on his cock, making him harder. He throbbed under her touch, which just made her even more hungry for him.

She held nothing back. She covered him with her saliva. He panted, hunched over, massaging her shoulders and begging her not to stop.

And then she tasted a hint of salty with the sweet. She pulled back, and a long string of precum attached itself to her mouth from the tip of his cock. She touched the tip and lifted the string onto her finger. And then she licked her finger tip and swallowed.

She dove right back for more, almost taking him in entirely. An inch short. And she tried for more. She gagged, spit on him, and tried again.

He pushed her away.

"Hold on," he said.

"To what?" she said.

"Your ass," he said, and reached for the condom. He unwrapped it, and slipped it on.

"I'd rather hold onto other things." She pushed him down on his back and straddled him. The expression on his face was priceless. He must've thought he'd be in charge at this point. He didn't object. He certainly didn't say no.

Candy slipped his tip inside her. Only the tip at first. That was all she could handle. She wiggled her hips, putting those belly dancing classes from long ago to good use. Slowly, she spread open for him. Even more slowly, she took in more of him. He massaged her sides and tugged at her bra straps.

And then, she had him balls deep. She felt so full, so stretched out. Amazing.

She rocked back and forth on him, as if riding a slow moving bull. She pressed her hands on his firm chest, squeezing his pec muscles. He played with her ass. To her surprise and delight, he pressed the tip of one finger into her bum, which made her feel all the more filled.

Somewhere along the way, her bra straps slipped down her shoulders. Her hair felt sweaty and sticky. It seemed like somebody turned up the room temperature by ten degrees, her skin felt so hot.

And then she rode him faster. Her world narrowed down to only him and the bed and the crazy good sensations coursing through her body. Her heart pumped overtime. The sounds of skin slapping against skin might've been coming from another room, made by some other couple doing far nastier things to each other.

She really wanted her bra off. But apparently, he didn't. And she was too busy fucking his brains out to bother with a clasp.

He renewed his fingering effort on her ass. And then he added a finger on her clit. Right when he did so, Candy let out the loudest scream she had ever heard come from her mouth.

And then she orgasmed on top of Brad.

She collapsed onto his arms. He held her, and inch by inch he slid out of her. She let out her breath when he was finally all the way out.

He rolled her over onto her back and straddled her.

To her shock, he reached for the bag of candy.

"You're still hard," she said.

"Not for long," he winked, eating a candy. And then dropping a few between her breasts.

She laughed and called him a dork.

Brad smiled so cutely when he pulled off his condom and tossed it aside. He didn't stop smiling while he jerked himself in front of her. Candy pressed her boobs together. He slipped his cock between them.

And then he titty fucked her.

Any other man, Candy might've found the experience boring. What would be the point? But after the orgasm he gave her, she couldn't deny him whatever he wanted. He made sexy grunting sounds while he jabbed his hips at her. Her entire body rocked with his motion. The bed squeaked. The headboard rattled.

He jerked himself a few times. He squeezed his thighs around her. And then stream after stream of sticky white come sprayed out of his cock. Candy didn't think it would ever stop.

When it finally did, he bent down and licked his mess up. He couldn't get it all, there was so much sprayed all over her.

He laid his head down between her breasts.

"When's the next date night?" Candy asked.

"Who said tonight's date was over?" he said, sounding as if half asleep.

Sounded like she needed to bang him again, before she missed her next opportunity. That would be the story of her life.

But she could afford to let him rest for a bit.

SPEED DATING NIGHT

TOO CRAZY...

*B*ryan Bachelor promised Phil, his coworker and occasional after work buddy, to go speed dating tonight. After three rounds, Bryan had too much merlot and not enough havarti cheese and ritz crackers. But all the alcohol in the world wasn't enough to loosen him up.

The woman across from him was cute, if a tad desperate. She wore a low-cut white blouse with a black bra underneath. Her makeup was layered on so heavy, she was three steps short of being a circus clown. An attractive version of Mimi from the Drew Carey Show, but with an annoying snort in her laugh every time she told a joke. Bryan pretended to laugh too.

Her perfume mingled with the potpourri of perfumes and colognes in the bar. It was like a candle shop, but more dangerous to the sinuses. The lovely expensive smells mixed with the cheaper, gas station variety perfumes. The result was a mishmash that was worse than any individual odor. Bryan sunk his nose into his wineglass, just to have a little relief.

Every five seconds, he glanced from Mimi's small and

perky rack to the massive digital clock on the stage, counting down the minutes to the next switch. Only three minutes. He could survive. But then the timer would start again. This was a long night already. Phil already scored on his first round, and left with his arm around a blond woman's shoulders (she wore tight black leather pants) and her hand on his ass. Lonely, and more than a tad jealous, Bryan kept his head low and tried to ignore the flood of other speed daters. At least it was an even mix of men and women. He'd worried there'd be too many women desperate for company and sex. Or worse, the event would be a sausage-fest.

He'd had no idea what to expect. Were there a lot of single people in the big city? Did they really spend Friday nights speed dating? The answers to those questions were yes, and what-the-fuck yes.

The bar itself was posh and cozy, more of a British-style pub than an American place. The massive mirror behind the bar made the crowd seem even larger, a sea of strangers drowning their loneliness with one free drink and a little company to numb the sting of being single. The maroon colored carpet was littered with broken peanut shells.

The heavy, dark varnished wood chair creaked every time Bryan shifted his butt a little. When he opened his mouth, he only managed a creak before Mimi prattled off another slapstick comment, and then he pretended to laugh again. Which only made her laugh even louder, as if she were trying to break his wineglass with her high-pitch squeal.

He had no idea what Mimi's real name was. The sticker name-tag pressed against her left boob was indecipherable. Maybe an E, or a J, the rest was round and flowing scribbles. Bryan certainly wasn't telling her what his last name was, for fear of what joke she might make.

Finally the clock's alarm dinged like a microwave. Time with Mimi was up. The event MC, a flamboyant man in a perfectly tailored tuxedo and greased back hair, grabbed the microphone and announced the time was up, as if the alarm wasn't enough notice.

Bryan waved goodbye to Mimi and zoomed off to the next table for his next date. She was a blond. The next one down was a brunette. After that was a redhead.

A little of everything, at least. He just wanted the night to be over.

Mimi screeched goodbye, and then swallowed the next sucker with a nasally laugh.

Bryan sat down in front of the blond. Her name-tag read Olivia in large sweeping cursive, and she had drawn three little hearts underneath. Her hair was curly and frizzy, and stuck out as if she had just rolled out of bed. She wore a loose hot pink tank top that revealed just about every mole on her tanned chest. As far as Bryan could tell, Olivia wore no bra. Her teacup sized breasts poked through the fabric of her shirt, hinting at the nipples.

She extended her hand out for Bryan to kiss, five shiny and mismatched bracelets on her wrist jingled. She kept her other hand under the table. Her beer glass was drained, only the suds left.

Bryan introduced himself, but only squeezed her hand. He tried to pull his hand back, but she held on. Be friendly, he reminded himself. Don't look at the clock. Oops, too late for that.

Something about this woman's perfume smelled off. Musty, actually. Then just below the constant din and rattle of the bar-life, Bryan heard a vibration.

He casually rubbed the inside of his ear with a pinky finger. Maybe Mimi damaged his eardrums.

Olivia clutched at his hand, squeezing tighter than he liked. She leaned forward, giving him a great view of her breasts, all the way to the pink nipples. Her face brightened red, thick lips rounded in an "o" and her eyes fluttering fast.

Her other hand was still under the table.

Bryan reconsidered what that vibrating sound might be.

"So, Olivia," he said. "What's your favorite music?"

She licked her lips. "Oh, anything hot and heavy."

"Such as?"

"Something that makes my hips shake."

"Okay." Bryan wanted to take his hand away, but that felt wrong. At the same time, he wanted to say something sexy, but that seemed too cheap. He always thought speed dating meant a lot of short dates with lots of people all in one night.

Apparently Olivia took speed dating to mean another thing. Cut all the crap with dating, and go straight to the big orgasm, without even bothering to figure out who's place to go to.

Bryan cleared his throat, and took another sip of merlot.

"You're cute," Olivia said. She muscled his hand closer to her chest. Not like it took a lot of strength, she could've punched Bryan and knocked his lights out, his defenses were so low. "I mean, really cute."

"Umm, thanks," he said.

The vibration under the table sped up a notch, and then another. Olivia's eyebrows fluttered and she rolled her eyes into the back of her head.

"So," Bryan said, "what are your hobbies?"

After a shudder that jiggled her hair about her face, she refocused. "I like hard hobbies. Long and hard."

"The kind that require double A batteries, clearly," he said, more to himself than to her.

"Don't get me wrong," Olivia said. "I like the real thing too. But it's not like I can carry a real one inside me everywhere."

"And the real one doesn't vibrate twenty-four seven."

"Exactly!" She squeezed his hand even tighter now. Another orgasm shuddered through her body, her shoulders bunching up, chest turning bright red.

The smell of wet pussy was embarrassing, and at the same time intoxicating. Like a bad joke that you should be ashamed of every time it's told, but then you tell it anyways. Bryan was disgusted, ashamed, and turned on by Olivia's behavior.

His prick told him so. And the equipment never lied about what turned Bryan on.

"So," he said. "You want to get out of here?"

Olivia clucked her tongue and shook her head. "If I said yes to that question for every guy, I'd never get to leave my bedroom."

"Fair enough. But come on, you gotta say yes to some lucky bastard here."

"Oh, you're sweet," Olivia said. "I don't have to go home with anyone to get off. Speaking of..." She scrunched her brows tight, and lowered her head onto the table, hair covering her face, a tiny moan escaped her throat.

Bryan rubbed his thumb over the back of her hand. "But there must be something I can do to convince you."

She raised her head slow. "Well, there is something. But you might not like it."

"You don't know. Hit me up."

Olivia took her hand away from his grasp. She sat upright, with one arm behind her head, the vibrator still doing its magic down below. "You have to lick my armpits."

"What? Wait..." Well at least her pits were shaved, but still.

"If it's my pussy you want in your face, and my nipples in your mouth, and my ass pressed against your pelvis." She poked her tongue out and licked her own underarm. She giggled, and looked straight at Bryan. "If you want all that, then you can lick my armpits."

"I… I don't know what to say to that."

The vibrator cut off. Olivia crossed her arms over her chest. The hand that had been doing the deed was slick and shiny.

"Is this negotiable?" said Bryan.

"Nope," Olivia said. "And our time's up anyway."

The giant ridiculous alarm clock buzzed.

"But…" Damn, he wanted her, and Bryan didn't know why. The crazy ones were always bad choices, and sitting across from a bad choice, he figured he could live with the consequences.

"Nope," she said again, looking away and flipping her hair to cover her face.

Bryan stood up slow, afraid of showing the world his massive erection. It was gone. Just as well.

The brunette waited at the next table.

ryan glanced over his shoulder, to make sure Olivia just wasn't playing hard to get. She already had one hand between her legs again, and was focused on the next poor bastard. Oh well.

Not only had she gotten him rock hard while only touching his hand, he had a little precum inside his underwear. The tip of his pecker was wet and a tad uncomfortable, and now he was determined to get laid here. He could do this.

The brunette tight-lip smiled as Bryan sat down. She was pretty, with straight shoulder length hair and an oval shaped face with high cheekbones. Her name-tag read Melissa, in simple all-cap block letters. She wore a light blue turtleneck shirt with long sleeves, baggy enough to cover her shape without looking sloppy. No earrings, bracelets, or rings. The only jewelry on her was a standard Citizen watch. Next to the gigantic yellow leather purse was an untouched lime soda drink with no ice. The bendy straw was in backwards, with the bent side touching the bottom of the glass.

The ridiculous clock was wound, and started ticking.

Melissa's smile persisted, as if she weren't sure what to do with her lips now that Bryan had sat down. Friendly, but not warm. A tad fake.

He folded his hands on the table in front of him, The dating jitters felt a little more real, now he was turned on. The possibility—the hope, really—that he was ending the night rolling around in the sack with somebody was real.

"Hi," said Bryan.

Melissa parroted the response, and then fidgeted with her watch.

Well, this was a great start.

"What're your favorite hobbies?" Bryan said, looking her in the eye and smiling back at her. He made his smile sharp and toothy, just enough to be sexy and toned down enough he could be friendly if things turned out wrong. Maybe she was tired of getting Olivia's castaways, and just needed some proper warming up. She made no response, except to sip from her soda. Well, shit, Bryan could've thought of a better opening line.

Melissa shrugged. She looked away, and took another dainty sip from her soda. "I like horses," she said at last.

"Awesome," he said. "You enjoy riding?"

"All the time."

Bryan had no idea if she was being cute or serious. He hoped for the former, prepared for the latter. "What do you like about riding?"

Maybe he should've added the word "horses" to the end of that phrase. Melissa didn't seem to notice the gentle double meaning. Her face was a perfect mask, with a cute mouth and a button nose. Could he give her a good time? Did he want to?

She seemed a little spacey for a moment, and then refocused on Bryan. "I like the freedom," she said at last. "The wind in my hair. A beautiful creature beneath me."

"So you like riding outdoors?" Bryan made the words sound serious, but with a curl in his smile in case she really did get the double meaning.

Melissa tilted her head and stared at him funny. "I rode PJ around the stadium during 4H. But that's not really the same."

Alright then.

"Do you do bareback riding?" he asked, fishing for something nice to say. He instantly regretted the phrasing.

"Oh, no," Melissa shook her head. The way her hair flitted about her forehead was kind of cute. "That's dangerous."

"I see," Bryan said. "But doesn't the idea sound fun? A wild animal between your legs, with a hint of danger?"

"I'm not sure what your idea of fun is," Melissa said, matter of factly.

"I'm not sure either, some days."

She took a long careful sip from her soda. The silence hung like an awkward… fuck it, Bryan had no word for how awkward this speed date was. He knew he had his own struggles at coming up with things to say. But Melissa just wasn't helping at all.

Instead of feeling attraction or lust, Bryan felt sorry for her. The mood was dead.

He reached out, grabbing both her wrists. After some fumbling, he held her hands in his.

"Melissa," Bryan said. "You're a beautiful woman."

"Thank you." She visibly brightened. "You're not bad yourself."

Bryan bit his lip, and then gave her the best sexy glare he could come up with. She leaned forward a little, blushing at the cheeks and neck.

"You'll find a wonderful man," he said. "Maybe even tonight, who knows. Although," he glanced to one side and whispered, "be careful with the men Olivia there is throwing away."

"Huh…" said Melissa, with a quick look at the blond woman. Olivia was still masturbating while holding a poor schmuck's hand. The new guy was visibly nervous, red as a beet and staring a hole in the table. "You know, all the guys tonight have been a little weird. No offense."

"My point is," Bryan said, "just be yourself. Mr. Right will be attracted to who you are."

"You're such a sweet man." She untangled one hand out of his, then grabbed the straw in her soda and took a sip. Her eyes zipped back to the guy at Olivia's table. "You think he's into horses?"

Bryan patted her on the hand. "You'll have to ask him. Maybe he has a hobby you'd enjoy."

"Like what?"

"Umm," Bryan said. The alarm clock dinged and the MC announced the time.

Bryan wished Melissa a wonderful night, and moved on to the next table. The redhead waited.

JUST RIGHT...

*B*ryan thought her name-tag was indecipherable at first. Curvy lines and scribbles that made no sense. But when he sat down, he cocked his head and realized the tag was on upside down.

Linda was the redhead's name. He introduced himself. After the pleasantries, they stared into each other's eyes and fell silent.

Not awkward. Bryan liked looking into her beautiful brown eyes. Linda had her hair tied in a loose ponytail, and wore eyeliner, lipstick, and only enough blush to give her pale skin some color. Her purple tank top fit snug around her body, making her hand-size breasts look bigger than what they probably were. She had an easy smile, and looked him straight back in the eyes.

She was fit without being too skinny. He wanted to see her standing up, but he imagined her having nice, shapely thighs and hips.

"I'd ask what your hobbies are," said Bryan, "but I feel like I've asked that a thousand times tonight."

"Ha," she snorted. She twirled a lock of hair with one

finger. "Don't bother. I keep changing my answers to that question."

"Fair enough," he said. "Let's put it this way. What would you rather do than speed date tonight?"

"Honestly? I'd probably be binging on '90s sitcoms. You know, Seinfeld. Home Improvement."

"Drew Carey?"

Linda snapped her fingers and bounced up and down in her seat. "Damn it! I miss Drew Carey! I loaned out my DVD collection to a friend and never saw them again."

Now here was a woman Bryan could appreciate. Someone who understood old references and liked classic shows. He leaned forward on his elbows. He bit his cheek, knowing he should keep his expectations in check. But deep down, he was excited for no explainable reason.

"I've got all the seasons," he said. He paused, and rubbed his chin. "Might be a little premature, but you're welcome to borrow them. Or, you know, come over and watch them."

Linda glanced at him askance, her eyes roaming up and down his body. "I'm sure we can come to an arrangement."

Bryan laughed a little. He couldn't help it. "So why aren't you binge watching '90s shows tonight? Instead of this."

Trying to beat the stupid giant clock, he wanted to say.

As if reading his mind, she shot a glance at the giant ridiculous alarm clock. Linda shrugged one cute bare shoulder. "A friend dragged me to this. And then she had the balls to leave me high and dry, when she hooked up with a tall, swanky stud."

This time, Bryan and Linda laughed together. "Same story here," he said. "My buddy left with a cute blond."

"Was she poured into a pair of tight leather pants?" Linda asked.

"Yeah," Bryan said slowly. "And she looked real comfortable with Phil."

"That was my friend Gloria."

"The same who has Drew Carey hostage?"

"You got it." Linda sighed. "I keep her around because I usually get lucky when she takes me out on the town."

"Any luck tonight?"

"Maybe."

He touched her on the back of the hand. Just a light touch, which turned into hand holding. Linda had nice warm hands, smooth as warm sateen. He imagined what it'd be like to have her hands on his body.

"So," Bryan said. "Our friends ditched out extra early. Want to follow their lead?"

"I follow nobody's lead," Linda leaned forward, giving him a nice view of her cleavage. "But I think we're both done here."

Bryan didn't need to be told twice. He stood up, then walked around to her side of the table and helped her up. Linda tucked her hand inside his elbow, and they walked right past the stupid clock and out the door.

He kissed her on the ear and said, "Your place or mine?"

"My apartment is empty," she said. "And it's across the street."

"Works for me," Bryan said. He felt light headed and more than a bit dizzy with excitement. Disbelief creeped into the back of his mind. Was this really happening? Was it really this simple with Linda? The traffic light wouldn't change fast enough.

When it did, Linda had no problem keeping up with his quick steps. She kept glancing at him and squeezing his arm. Once they were across the street, she kissed him on the shoulder.

Then she pointed to a flower store on the corner. "Above that shop," she said.

Linda opened the side door with a key on a dangly chain,

and led him upstairs a narrow flight of stairs. At the top, she turned back to him.

She smiled shyly. Cute as hell, but Bryan sensed a problem. "Is it okay if I have second thoughts?"

"We just met," he said. "Sure, I'd be disappointed, but you're the lady in charge."

"Do you have a condom?"

"Yes."

"Came prepared to speed dating?"

"A man has to hope," he said, shrugging. "We can just binge watch TV and see how the night ends."

"Sounds like a dangerous plan," she said. "I like it."

Linda unlocked her apartment door and yanked Bryan inside. She wasn't lying when she said it was empty. Calling her place a studio was being generous. Just a small room with white painted walls, shaggy green carpet that might've been left over from the '80s, and a kitchenette in one corner. Under the one window was a futon on the floor. Opposite from that was a big screen TV.

"Nice place," he said.

She shut the door behind her. "Don't be coy."

"Really, I like this. Simple, to the point. My kind of woman."

Linda flopped down on the futon and flicked on the TV. She patted the spot next to her. Bryan set his keys, wallet, and phone beside the futon and sat next to her. He put his arm around her shoulders. To his pleasant surprise, she snuggled right in.

She turned on Seinfeld.

This was definitely the strangest speed dating night he'd ever done. Not what he expected.

Bryan hoped the night wasn't over yet.

*A*fter five episodes of Seinfeld, Bryan had to push Linda off, because his arm was falling asleep. She had been still the entire time, with her head nestled in the crook of his neck and her elbow temptingly close to his crotch. He was hard from the opening segment of the first episode to the end credits of the last. He rubbed her arms now and then. His fingers were so close to her breasts, he wanted to lightly pinch a nipple to see how she'd react.

But Bryan played the gentleman and enjoyed the shows. Not difficult to do, because he was honestly enjoying the evening with Linda.

He made a show of rubbing blood back into his arm. "Should we call it a good night? Or you up for more?"

"It's already been a good night," she said. "How about we make it a wonderful night?"

Bryan liked the sound of that. He smoothed her red hair behind her ears. Cupping her face, he brought her closer.

Then he kissed her. He prepared for a quick smooch, hoped for a lot more. At first it was only a meeting of lips.

Bryan pressed his tongue against her teeth. Just the tip, to test the waters. Linda grabbed him by the shirt sleeves and climbed on top of him, straddling her legs around him.

She jabbed her tongue in his mouth. He slipped his arms around her waist, and reached around to cop a feel. Linda had a firm, bubbly ass. The feel turned into a squeeze. He couldn't quite force himself to let go. She tugged him by the hair and continued making out with him.

And then she shook her hips. Bryan was uncomfortably hard. No way she didn't notice him poking at her.

He grabbed the bottom of her ass, bringing her body heat as close as possible. He was frustrated by her skinny jeans. He wanted to press a finger into her folds and explore every inch.

Linda carefully unbuttoned his shirt, one painstaking button at a time. The love making was slow, sweet, and bothersome like an itch that couldn't be scratched. Eventually, Linda stripped Bryan to the waist and tossed his shirt aside. She lightly scratched him across the shoulders and down the chest. He lifted her shirt. Her skin was baby smooth.

Linda stopped the kissing abruptly, leaving him panting for more. Crossing her arms at the waist, she lifted her shirt the rest of the way and pulled it off, revealing her black bra.

Bryan held her at arm's length for a moment, just to enjoy the view. She ran her fingers through her own hair, beaming a smile that was too precious for words, like an angel sitting on his lap.

"I didn't expect speed dating to end like this," he said.

"Nobody does," Linda said, a crafty quirk lifting in her brows. Before Bryan could make a lame joke about the Spanish Inquisition, she tugged at his belt.

They hastily removed each others' pants. Kissing, scratching, pinching the entire time. He removed his briefs and black socks. She did the work of taking off her own panties.

And then she pushed him flat onto the futon. Then she straddled her legs around his head, shoving her neatly trimmed pussy to his mouth, and went down on him. She teased his tip with her wet tongue. Bryan didn't need much encouragement. He held her by the hips, and lapped at her folds.

With two fingers, he opened her and licked at her exposed clit. She was already wet and tasted sweet. Linda had him by the balls and licked him up and down the shaft.

He dived two fingers inside her, which forced a cute squeal out of her. Her tunnel was pleasantly tight and slick. Bryan felt around inside, curling his fingers slowly. Linda tensed up and then relaxed lazily top of him. She swallowed his cock, breathing heavily through her nose, but every time he tickled her G-spot, she stopped sucking and only rubbed her tongue across him.

And then her pussy contracted. Linda gag screamed around his cock, and a small gush came out of her pussy. She sat upright, pussy pressing down gently on his face as she wiggled around. Bryan lapped at her juices.

Linda rolled off of him. She was faced away, giving him a nice view of her bubbly ass. One of her bra straps had fallen down. She panted, and half turned to him. Her face and chest were bright red with exertion. "Oh my," she said, cupping a hand to one breast.

Bryan sat up and moved toward her, grabbing her by the waist. She didn't resist. He pulled down the other bra strap and kissed her on the shoulder. He reached around her for his wallet, and got the condom. A minute later, he was ready for more adventure.

Then he bent Linda over and rubbed her pussy to get her wet all over again. She didn't take much coaxing. She white-knuckle gripped the edge of the futon with both hands.

He plunged his cock inside her. A perfect fit. Tight

without being uncomfortable. He shook his hips Elvis-style. Linda squirmed and squealed underneath him. The temperature of the apartment seemed to heat up another five degrees. Bryan's skin was hot and tingly. Sweat pored down his back. Linda was hot and sweaty too. Her hair was tangled and falling over her face.

He clutched her hips, holding her still. Then he pounded her as hard and fast as he could. If her neighbors were home, they almost certainly heard the skin on skin slapping sounds. Surely they also heard Linda's moans and half muffled screams. They probably heard Bryan smacking Linda's ass hard enough to leave a handprint.

Maybe Bryan should've left the TV on.

But he wasn't about to remedy that. A little part of him enjoyed the thrill of being caught.

Linda turned her head around, a pleading look in her expression. Her makeup was a mess. So was her hair.

Tension built up in his balls. There was no stopping it.

A wild idea popped up in his brain.

Right as he was about to blow, he pulled out. He snapped the condom off. Bryan barely had to stroke himself. He popped a creamy load on her back, stream after stream. Just kept coming. So much he wasn't sure if his orgasm would end.

When it did, he collapsed face down on Linda's futon. She fell on top of him.

"Why did I avoid speed dating for so long?" he said.

She kissed him on the nape of the neck. "And you can keep avoiding it now," she said.

"Good," he said. Bryan liked the way Linda teased her fingers across his ribs. He also liked how her leg was pressed into his crotch. He fell asleep with her on top of him. When he woke up, she was no longer there. But he heard the shower running.

And that was the end of speed dating, and the beginning of the best sex in Bryan's life.

FIVE YEARS WITHOUT DESSERT

THE BEST FRIDAY NIGHT

On a whim Caleb Nelson placed his hand on top of Michelle's. He wanted to do that all night, and thought about it all day before their date.

The waitress just brought cherry pie a la mode for both of them. Rock music played from the other side of the wall in the kitchen, almost loud enough to drown out the cooks' bantering, the heavy rhythm an annoying counter-point to the softer pop music playing from the dining room's speakers.

Hardly anybody was at Betty's Stackhouse at ten o'clock in the evening. It was like the world had gone quiet and stayed home. Either that or Betty's was going out of business. Judging by the potholes in the parking lot and the funky smells in the bathroom, that wouldn't have surprised him.

Just Caleb and Michelle, and an older couple who ordered heavenly smelling blueberry pancakes. Caleb almost wished he'd split an order of that with Michelle, instead of the pie.

She wrapped her fingers around his and clasped her other hand over his. She had the most amazing green eyes that lit up when she smiled at him. Her long black hair was tied up in a loose bun, the green and purple dyed strands hung down in front of her ears. She wore a pink cardigan over a white and black stripped dress.

Under the table, every so often, she bumped her ankle boot against his calf, especially when making a point.

"Your pie smells delicious," she said, bumping into his calf.

"So does yours," Caleb squeezed her fingers gently.

He almost hadn't chosen Betty's. Almost hadn't gone out with Michelle for the second time this week. Their first date had been impromptu after work on Monday. Just coffee between coworkers, nothing more. And that's what Caleb figured it would remain, despite how wonderful that made the beginning of the week feel.

Until Michelle texted him early in the morning, while he was still eating his bagel and on the first cup of coffee for the day, and asked him what he was doing. He called her, and asked her to meet him for pie either later tonight or on Friday.

Michelle immediately responded, "Tonight."

Betty's was a choice of habit. Despite the mediocre service and the smelly bathrooms, they had the best pies in town.

He relaxed his fingers out of her hands, and she let go. As she dug into her pie, he poured fresh coffee for both of them.

"I'd ask how your day was," he said.

Michelle giggled. "Rule number three."

"Right," he said. Three simple rules they'd made up and agreed to before their first date. Rule three was to never ask about work outside of work. Since it was still Friday, and they both worked at an IT call center, Caleb already figured how her day went.

She wiggled her spoon at him. "You did forget to ask me something."

Caleb poured creamer into her coffee and stirred it. Funny how he knew her preferences, like they were already a couple—one creamer, no sugar. He took the exact opposite, preferring sweetness over taste.

"What's that?" he said, trying to hide his smile and failing. He honestly figured he lost his chance after their Monday night date. Having a second chance so soon was a pleasant surprise.

"You forgot?" she said. Michelle glanced at him askance, then shook her head, the green and purple strands jiggling about. "Well then, you'll have to figure it out for yourself."

"Well crap," he said.

And then she laughed at him. He could've watched her laugh all night if it were possible. The way one eye slitted almost shut, the other widened. The quirky way her lips curled. And the cute pink blush on her ears and throat.

They chatted about nothing and everything while they ate pie and drank coffee. Books, movies, concerts they'd love to see. He stacked her empty plate on top of his and shoved them aside. Then he poured more coffee for her.

"Slow down there, buddy," Michelle said. "You want me up all night?"

"Maybe I do," Caleb said, winking. He added another creamer to hers, a sugar to his, and stirred both.

"Good thing I don't work tomorrow," she said. "And if I did, I might not care."

"Is that so?"

"Depends on what your intentions are," she said with that funny quirk in her lips.

"I... I don't know," he said. He stared down at his mug, not sure how to say what he needed to say to her. After an appropriately awkward silence, he blurted it out. "It's been a long time since I've done this."

"This?" she said. Then she took his hand in hers. "Sex? Or dating? Just asking."

"Both," he said. "The last time was a date like this. Too much coffee, a sugary dessert, and we ended the night rolling around in bed."

"May I ask how long ago?" she said. "Not my business if you don't want to tell me."

"Five years," he said.

Caleb expected her to take her hand away from his. Maybe recoil in shock. Or pity. She did none of those things.

Instead, she massaged his thumb with hers. "Sorry to hear that," she said, and sounded like she meant it.

"Nothing to be sorry for," he said. "I told you about my bookstore? I got busy building a business and had so little time for anything serious. Nothing unserious came along either."

"Nothing wrong with a focused man," she said.

"And then the recession happened and I lost everything," he said.

"Nothing wrong with that either," she said. "I lost a six-figure corporate job and moved back in with my parents for three years. Talk about not having dessert."

"Not having dessert?" Caleb said.

Michelle chuckled. When she talked to him, often she got ahead of herself in conversations. Caleb suspected this was one of those times.

Rule number two—always ask for clarification before assuming. A good rule. One Caleb wished he'd had with previous girlfriends.

"Your last girlfriend," she said. "You had dessert and then sex. You haven't done that in five years."

"Gotcha." Caleb nodded his head. And then laughed. Five years without dessert seemed like a damn long time when Michelle put it like that.

She cocked her head to one side, letting the multi-colored locks of hair fall across her shoulder. "Just saying, you should allow yourself some dessert now and then."

"I just had cherry pie. Not sure what you mean by that." Caleb patted her forearm. She brushed him aside.

"I think you know what I mean," she said. "If you knew what to ask me about."

He smiled. Caleb hadn't forgotten of course. Just put it off, unsure if he was ready. If not now, then when? Ever? Fuck it...

"Do you want to come back to my place for a night cap?" he asked.

"I do," she said, bumping him in the leg with her boot.

He allowed the moment to sink in. At last, after all this time working so hard with no play, Caleb finally had a shot. He wasn't going to force things to happen, but a chance was a chance. But he still needed one thing.

"You sure about this?" he said. "Could get complicated at work. Not like I'm trying to blow my own chances or anything."

Michelle nodded slowly, smiling. "And if it gets complicated? I don't know, I'm due for another job soon. We'll figure it out. Besides, you violated rule number one."

"Oops," he said. "I won't make that mistake again."

Rule number one... see rule number three.

They laughed together, holding hands. He leaned forward and kissed her on the mouth. Michelle leaned toward him to get closer. She licked his teeth and played with his tongue. Caleb became uncomfortably hard. He wanted to adjust himself, or better yet let himself out.

Once the kiss ended, he stared into her eyes for a long time. Michelle cupped his face with both hands. He held her by the elbows. Only the table was in the way. The moment could've gone on forever.

"I'll text you my address," he said.

"Sounds good," she said. "Just bring a condom."

"Thought of that earlier today."

"Oh?" she said. "Somebody likes to be prepared."

"I live fifteen minutes from here," he said.

"Good. I can't wait much longer."

He scooped up the bill, tossed a five on the table for the waitress, and went to pay.

His boner hadn't gone down. The waitress certainly noticed, though he tried to cover it with his jacket. But he felt too good to care what she thought.

Tonight was the best Friday night he'd had in a long time.

THE PERFECT NIGHT

Caleb barely shut the front door behind him when Michelle grabbed the back of his hair and kissed him again. He pressed her up against the wall, hands on her waist, tongue in her mouth. She felt small in his arms, like she was made to fit inside him. Much smaller than he imagined. Working with her, seeing her as an equal made her seem larger than life. Now she was flesh and blood and in his home.

She still smelled of coffee and pie. Her perfume was faded now, just a hint of chamomile and lilacs.

He made out with her in the front hall. It'd been so long since he'd done this with a woman in this spot, it felt unreal and amazing at the same time. Like a dream, but lucid. He kept expecting to snap out of it any time, and come back to reality.

And then he picked her up in his arms. She giggled and wrapped her arms around his neck, holding on loosely. That was reality enough for him.

He carried her upstairs to his bedroom. Luckily he left the bedside lamp on and pulled down the covers just for this occasion. Funny how he hadn't expected this, but prepared for it anyway.

And then he tossed her onto his bed. Michelle bounced a couple times.

"I'll get the nightcaps," he said. "What's your poison?"

Michelle pressed a finger under her lip. "My poison? You, of course."

Caleb liked the sound of that. He took his shirt off and climbed onto the bed with her. Her fingers were all over his skin, up his ribs, lazily across his nipples, down his stomach. He worked out, but hadn't been particularly proud of his progress. By the whimsical expression on Michelle's face and her hungry fingers, she had no complaints about his physique.

He nudged her down flat on the bed. Michelle pulled the pins out of her bun, letting her hair fall apart around her. He toyed with her hair, his fingers combing through her mane.

"I think I love you," he said.

"Stop thinking already and do something about it," she said.

He kissed her on the neck. Thrashing about, she managed to take off her cardigan, breaking a few seams along the way, and tossed it aside on the floor. His kisses went down her neck, her shoulder, down her bare arm. He kissed all the way to her wrist. And then back up her other wrist, repeating the motion in reverse.

One knee between his legs, she tickled his ribs, making him stop and gasp.

"Ticklish?" she said as if sorry, but not.

"Damn it," he said, "you figured it out."

Michelle giggled. "Damn it all."

She focused her fingers on other parts. Across his back, His shoulder blades. Just above his belt. Her fingers roamed everywhere, as if she wanted to touch everything all at once.

And then she pushed at him to let her up. She turned around, presenting the zipper on the back of her dress. He slowly unzipped her and let the dress fall down around her waist. He helped her out of it and tossed it aside on the bed. She wore a black bra and matching panties and her boots. Nothing else, besides her earrings and necklace.

Caleb admired her for a moment. For as long as he'd worked with her, he so often fantasized about having her in his bed like this. Now that fantasy became reality, he wondered again if he'd wake up.

And if he did, he wanted to make the most of this crazy ass dream.

He kissed down her shoulder and back, casually tugging down one bra strap as he followed the curve of her body. And then down further, across her bubble butt. With one finger, he pulled down her panties, revealing a neatly trimmed patch of hair between her legs. Her labia were shaved smooth.

Michelle leaned on her elbows, pointing her butt in the air to give him better access. Caleb traced his tongue across her lips. Gentle, slow. The smell of her pussy drove him insane. He'd forgotten what it felt like to do this. It was all he could do to keep himself in control, make it as pleasurable for her as possible. He wanted to be inside so badly. His heart hammered in his chest. He could barely keep his fingers from shaking in anticipation.

"Play with my clit too," she said, reaching between her legs to rub her clit as if to show him what she wanted. "Pretty please?"

Caleb couldn't say no to that.

He flicked his tongue across her clit, back and forth, up and down, varying the pace and the rhythm. He opened her labia up, pressed his tongue inside for a bit, before returning back to her clit. He wandered across all her parts.

And then while rubbing her clit with one finger, he used his other fingers inside her, curling them against her G-spot. Took a few minutes, but he figured out where she was sensitive. He still knew how to do the rip-and-grip technique, as his last girlfriend called it.

Thankfully, Michelle seemed to enjoy it more. She moaned in pleasure, begging him to not stop.

But he did.

Michelle protested. Caleb ignored her, and reached for the top nightstand drawer. The box of condoms were there, and he got one. She watched him the whole time, a big smile on her face, ass wiggling about.

Once he had the condom slipped on, he took her by the hips from behind. Then he teased her with the tip of his cock. And inch, then pulled out. A little further inside, making her squeal, then out again. Finally he entered her balls deep.

Caleb wiggled his hips about, repeatedly hitting and stroking her G-spot with the tip of his cock. Her juices dripped as if somebody poured warm water down his balls. He slowed to a stop, then continued. She mumbled incoherently, rubbing her clit with her finger as he fucked her. She rocked her hips against him to try to make him go faster.

He went faster. Then slowed down again. He kept varying the pace, making her squirm and beg.

And then he flipped her over onto her back. Caleb lifted Michelle's legs over his shoulders and entered her again. He closed her legs so she was tight on his cock.

Michelle gripped the bedsheets in her fists. Her chest heaved, pushing her breasts up in her bra. Her hair clung in sweaty strands on her face.

And then Caleb took her faster and harder. He shook the bed. His skin heated and he had a hard time breathing. His heart hammered in his chest.

She screamed out loud enough to wake up neighbors. Caleb didn't even care. So what if they heard? He didn't care what they thought. This was what he'd dreamed about for so long. And now he was having the best dessert and the best date he'd had in a very long time. The neighbors' opinions were a small price to pay for a beautiful night of action.

He felt the come building up in his balls. The orgasm was so close. But he denied himself the pleasure. He stopped, and then kissed and made out with her. Michelle grabbed his ass in both hand, slapping him hard as if to make start again.

He made her suffer with need. Just as much as he suffered for all those years without dessert. He wanted her body to ache just like his did. Ache with the desire to explode in pleasure with someone else.

And then he was dangerously close. Caleb pulled out and rolled onto his back, telling her he needed a break. But Michelle would have none of that.

She climbed on top of his reverse cowgirl style. She took him in gently, carefully. Once she was settled on top, she flipped her hair and looked over her shoulder at him. She smiled.

And then Michelle grabbed him by the thighs and bounced on top of him. Her bra came off. And then she took off her boots. The whole time she kept him inside her. Closer to the edge, desperate to have all of her, Caleb massaged her butt and begged her to make him come inside of her.

But before he did, her pussy spat him back out. Michelle ripped the condom off, almost tearing if apart. She took his cock into her mouth, tasting all of him from tip to balls and back up again.

He'd never blown a load with a blowjob, and wanted to tell her so. But he kept his mouth shut. He figured she'd give him some pleasant oral and then he could continue having her pussy wrapped around his cock again.

Except he felt the orgasm long before it hit fully. Her teeth applied pressure up and down his shaft. She massaged and tugged on his balls.

He came all over her face. Strings of come blew into her hair.

Exhausted and spent, Caleb stretched out on his back. Michelle settled on top of him, kissing his neck.

"How was dessert?" she said.

"Thank you," he said. "Perfect."

He couldn't say much more.

Five years was too long to wait. It felt like the first time all over again, but much sweeter. Michelle had been the perfect woman to share it with.

FOR FRIENDS AND MONEY

THE SETUP

*H*er heart fluttered to the bottom of her throat, and Abby swallowed it back down. Losing her paycheck money didn't bother her too much. The fantasy playing out in her head, and the thought of finally making it real, made her sweat.

Abby knew it was wrong. Full out, no question, absolutely and idiotically wrong. And maybe that's why she was at a casino in bumfuck, Nebraska, blowing cash on the slot machines. That might also explain why her ass and thighs were so sore.

She could barely sit in front of the slot machine, so she didn't spend very long at one. Win a little, lose everything, then pick up her twenty ounce bottle of orange soda, and walk about a bit before settling in to lose more money. She wandered over to the blackjack tables, gawked at the handsome dealer in his shiny black vest and starched white sleeves. Then wander back to the slots.

The pattern repeated itself.

The buffet beckoned. Abby longed for the cheesy biscuits, macaroni, and the wonderful apple pie with a cup of coffee.

She hadn't eaten in six hours, since the late breakfast of cold cereal at the hotel. But the jitters kept her away from the buffet.

Away from the him. The cute waiter with dark curly hair and olive tanned skin. He wasn't particularly tall, only her height if she wore heels. But Patrick made up for vertical challenge with charm.

He'd charmed her right out of her only pair of panties, in fact. And damn it, she was getting them back.

Abby walked from slot machine to slot machine, the cool air conditioning tickling her like gentle kisses between her legs. She'd never been so bravado like this. She wore a yellow sundress she'd bought at a local department store this morning, and wedge sandals to match. Why she hadn't bought new panties, Abby wasn't entirely sure. But the jeans and tank top she brought with her to Nebraska needed to be washed.

She needed money. Her cash ran low a day ago, and stupidly enough was running even lower. She didn't want to use her credit card too much, and she needed some money in reserve for gas on the way home. Next week's paycheck wouldn't come soon enough.

Her vacation started well enough. The break from managing the lingerie department had been a long time coming. The department was constantly short staffed with people who had no retail experience, and district managers were constantly berating Abby for everything that went wrong.

But all that was two states away, and she had one more night to do anything she wanted.

She finished off the last of the orange soda and threw away the bottle in the recycling. One walk through the gift shop told her she'd already spent enough money on souvenirs. And what she really wanted wasn't something she could buy, exactly.

Actually, it was something Patrick the waiter was going to buy.

Last night had been amazing. Chilled merlot with a plate of fancy cheeses. Each time he fed her a piece, Patrick told her what the cheese was called. By that point, Abby had been too drunk to pay much attention to anything besides the loose top button of his shirt. He kissed her at some point, and slowly made out with her. Right when she was ready to let him take her panties off, he led her outside to watch the fireworks show.

Luckily, she didn't have to wait very long. He got her panties off, along with every other stitch of clothing. He made love to her on the grass, banged her silly back in the hotel room, and then held her close for the rest of the night. Patrick kept her panties in the morning, and left her with a kiss on the cheek and a promise of more fun if she stopped by the buffet.

Abby took a deep breath, and stepped into the restaurant. The tables were mostly empty now, except for the late after-noon folks who ate long lunches, and the folks who ate early dinners.

And there he was. Patrick.

She wasn't sure why the nerves hit her. After all, she'd already been with this guy. Shouldn't that make things easier to ask for sex?

But the way he looked at with those dark eyes under those thick brows, how he seemed to be undressing her in his mind, just made her all the more nervous.

Abby picked a table in the corner, and sat down with her back to the wall. Patrick came over with a tall glass of orange soda, and sat down across from her.

"Hello friend," he said.

"Lover," she said. Abby unwrapped the straw he offered, slowly, and then took a long sip of the soda.

"Last night was wonderful," Patrick said, leaning forward with his elbows on the table. He glanced down the front of her dress. "I thought of you all day."

"Is that so?" She cupped her face with both hands. Their mouths almost touched.

"I want you again," he touched her on the elbows.

"This time," she said, licking her lips, "it's going to cost you."

"Oh?" He pulled away from her. Then his brows furrowed with curiosity. "Do you have a proposition?"

"As a matter of fact…" Her words were almost a whisper. He stared at her in concentration, as if every word were the most important thing ever. She smiled. "You know what they say. The first time you do it for your friends. The second time you do it for money."

He was silent for a moment. The wheels were turning in his head. She hoped he'd figure out what she meant, or at least ask enough questions. Abby wasn't sure how to explain what she wanted, she just knew in the pit of her stomach she wanted something no man had ever done for her.

And then Patrick smiled. "I see," he said. "We're not friends?"

"I don't think we can be," Abby said. "We live in different states, have different lives, and the only thing we have in common is lust. When I'm gone, you'll go back to your life, and I'll go back to mine."

"I'm sorry for that," he said.

"Don't be. You gave me a wonderful gift. Now I want one more thing."

His face and neck reddened. He leaned closer to her, and spoke very softly. "Good thing I made a lot in tips today. I'll need a lot of cash to pay for the services you'll provide me."

Abby giggled. She couldn't help it. "Then you understand what I want."

"You want to be a slut," he said. "Not just treated like one. To literally be one for a night."

"Yes," Abby placed a hand on her chest. "Oh God, yes."

Finally, her fantasy became real. She was so close to knowing what it was like to be a whore, and she had a good man to treat her like one for a night.

THE DEAL

*P*atrick insisted they take a walk first. Somewhere outside the bustle of the casino and hotel where they could talk realistically.

Abby mentioned the park behind the casino. Lots of benches, a small pond, and trees. The wind blew through her hair, cooling off the sweat on the back of her neck. The after-noon sun drifted lazily over the tree tops.

"You sure about this?" he said.

Abby wanted him to take her right now. She'd never been this excited, anxious, and nervous all at the same time. He could at least hold her hand, or touch her on the arm, or some-thing. But he kept cool and stayed a safe distance from her. Close enough to be friendly, but without invading her space.

"I've fantasized about this for a long time," she said.

"But I want to be clear about what you want," Patrick said. "What is your fantasy?"

She stopped in her tracks, and then sat down on the nearest park bench. How to explain this? Especially to a man. Would he understand? It was one thing to have the dream in her mind while she masturbated with her favorite vibrator, and tell the story to herself.

The story, of course, of how she was desperate for the money, and got reduced to selling her body. How she'd get used by a strange man.

It was so simple in her mind. So very hard to just open her mouth and tell him what she wanted.

Patrick sat down next to her. His body warmth touched her shoulder.

"Okay, I'll share my fantasy first," he said. "And I won't do this to you, if it doesn't appeal to you."

"Thank you." She slouched in the bench slightly, and tilted her head up at him. He had a sexy square jawline, perfect for kissing underneath as she discovered during last night's tryst. Last night he'd been cleaned shaved. Today, he had some fuzz. Clearly, she'd kept him up late enough that he hadn't cared about shaving this morning.

She couldn't believe this was really happening. A man she already trusted, and had little reason to, who was willing to role-play her fantasy.

Just the fact that he was entertaining the notion of making her a prostitute gave her hope. And then offering to share his own fantasy relaxed her a little.

But it took him awhile to share. He sat moving that sexy jaw for a bit. And then he smiled.

"So, don't laugh," he said. Patrick cleared his throat. "None of my girlfriends ever wanted to try this with me."

"I'm listening," Abby said, moving just a hair closer to him and his warm shoulder.

He shifted a little, and gave her a cute, somewhat dorky, smile. "I've always wanted to tie up and blindfold my woman. And then use her any which way I wanted to."

Abby laughed. But she hoped not in a mean way. He

turned his head. She quickly said, "And none of your girl-friends were willing to do that for you?"

"Nope," Patrick said. "It's stupid. I understand if you're not into that."

She touched him on the forearm. "I'd like you to do that to me," she said. "And I think it'll fit nicely into my fantasy."

"Oh, yeah?"

"Yeah," Abby said. "I wanted to be taken by a guy who pays me for my body. He doesn't want me for a girlfriend, doesn't buy me nice things. Just uses me and walks away."

"But as a role-play?" he said.

"Yes! Totally. Use me like I'm a pussy to be filled." Abby frowned at what she just said. She'd never put those words to the fantasy in her head, and it came out sounding like some-thing a guy would fantasize about. She laughed again. "But I insist on a condom, like last night."

"No problem," Patrick said. "And to be clear on some-thing. Umm..."

"Yes?" Abby tilted her head, and took him by the hand.

"Is this a rape fantasy?" he said quickly.

"No," she said. "And thanks for asking."

"Good," he said. "i'm not sure if I could've done that for you."

"I think that requires a whole 'nother level of trust," she said. "But maybe..."

"For tonight, you're a prostitute at the casino," Patrick said. "And I'm a John with too much money, looking for something he can't get at home."

"Perfect!" Abby dug through her purse. She handed him the magnetic hotel key for her room. "Take this. Pretend the room is yours. I can get a spare key from the front desk so I can still get if I need to."

"Feel free to take out any valuables from the room," he said.

"I got everything valuable in here," she patted her purse. "Which ain't much."

"How about a safe word?" he said. "In case I go too far and you need to stop me."

Abby tapped her chin. She'd thought about before, in her private fantasies. But now that it was really happening, her mind froze up. Patrick told her to just say the first thing that came to her mind.

"Fine," she said. "Jack rabbit."

She giggled at that, but he agreed to the safe word being "jack rabbit." Kind of appropriate, Abby thought, since they were about to do what rabbits did best.

He took her hand, a serious expression on his brows. "You sure about this?"

"Yes," she said, and then pecked him on the cheek. "Not sure if I can look the part. Didn't bring a lot of clothes with me, unfortunately."

Patrick dug into his pocket, and pulled out a brass money clip with a large wad of green. He counted out two hundred dollars. "Pair of shoes and a dress?" he said.

"I can't." Abby held her hands up. "That's too much."

"Come on," he said, shoving the money into her hand. "This is your night. And I'm getting excited about this, too."

"But that's a lot of money," she said.

"I've had a good summer with tips," he winked. "Besides, for my little slut, I'd pay anything to see her in some nice clothes, just to rip them off her."

Abby's breath caught. Her stomach fluttered and her heart skipped a beat. She took the money he offered.

For her John—Patrick—she was going to buy the best possible dress and shoes she could find with his money.

Even if he ruined them later tonight.

THE RIDE

She waited in the casino lobby, next to the red convertible that was part of some kind of raffle going on. Abby wore a red flowery sundress that showed off more of her legs than she was used to, and a pair of six-inch heel white pumps. She felt tall and strong, towering over even a lot of the men in the casino. And she got more than a few hot glances, from both sexes.

If only those people knew she wasn't wearing panties. That little secret gave her a thrill all its own, as if knowing that gave her some kind of superpower. It was silly, of course. She couldn't even explain it to herself. Just this strange high of being vulnerable and confident at the same time.

Abby was excited with jitters. Her hot skin prickled with gooseflesh. On the one hand, she should just wait for Patrick, on the other she could walk away, get in her car, and drive away forever.

But if she walked away, Abby knew she'd always wonder what might've happened.

She was staying, no matter how long it took him to show

up. And if he flaked out on her, that was his own dumbass fault.

And then Abby saw him. He wore a purple dress shirt with the sleeves rolled up, jeans, and shiny black dress shoes. His hair was neatly combed, but he still hadn't bothered to shave.

Patrick smiled at her as he walked up.

"Hello," he said. A hint of his cologne reached her. She hadn't noticed his dimples before, oddly. Her knees felt oddly weak. Certainly this wasn't how a hooker felt when approached by a client.

But then how would she know?

"Hi," she said. The silence simmered between them. Abby didn't know what to say next. Was she supposed to proposition him? Shit, she hadn't thought of that.

He glanced over both shoulders and shoved his hands in his pockets. Then he pointed towards the gift shop. "I, uh, noticed you from over there."

"Did you now?" she said.

"I'd like to buy you a drink," he said at last. He smiled, as if he'd thought of that line all night, and only now came up with the courage to say it.

"I'd like that."

He offered his hand, and walked her to the bar, where he bought two glasses of merlot. They chatted as if they didn't know each other already. What's your name? Where you from? What are you doing tonight? Another two rounds of wine went by.

The alcohol went to Abby's head. She leaned forward, her hand dangerously high up on his thigh. "If you mean to talk business," she said, "we should find somewhere more private."

"What do you mean?" he said with more than a hint of humor, and drunkenness, in his voice.

"I hope you brought money, sir," she hopped off the barstool and staggered away.

"My room?" Patrick said, following close behind, and caught her by the elbow before she could stumble into one of the cocktail waitresses.

"Don't be so hasty," Abby said. "But if you can afford me, we should head in that direction."

She let him lead her to the hotel, which was connected to the casino. At the elevators, he shoved her against the wall, and took out the money clip from his hip pocket.

Her eyes bulged wide at the wad of cash he had. How did a waiter, even a talented one at a busy casino, have that much cash on hand? She was stunned speechless. Abby didn't even hear what he said at first.

"How much are you worth, little slut?" he said brusquely. When she didn't answer, he counted out two hundred dollars and shoved it into her bra. "There. I hope that buys more than a sloppy blowjob in the elevator."

Once again, those dimples came out. He even blushed a little at what he said. Abby found that too cute for words.

"You can take me back to your room with that money," she said. "I might even spread my legs for you."

Patrick counted out another two hundred dollars and shoved it into the other cup of her bra. Then he pushed the elevator button. When the elevator dinged open, he grabbed her by the elbow, and dragged her in. He was rough, as if he didn't care if she wanted to go with him or not.

With four hundred bucks in her bra, Abby would've followed him to the roof. Forget the money, she'd fuck him on the roof anyway after seeing the slightly darker side of Patrick.

They were the only people in the elevator. He leaned with his back to the wall.

"How about that sloppy BJ?" he said. Before Abby could

answer, he placed a hand on her head, and shoved her down to her knees. Then he opened his pants in front of her face. Abby was pleased to see that he was going commando too.

Like a good whore, she wasted no time when he offered his half limp cock.

Abby took the tip in her mouth, rolling her tongue across him. Then she licked down to his balls and sucked them. She stroked his shaft. He raised to attention at her touch.

And then he grabbed her by the sides of her head, pushing her on his cock. Abby breathed through her nose, but she still felt suffocated by his musk and girth. At first, she tried to avoid using her teeth. Her jaw muscles became sore from the action, she had to relax her mouth. As she spat him back out, she scraped her teeth up his shaft.

"Good slut," he said.

Abby didn't wait for him to shove her face down again. She swallowed him whole, using all of her mouth. Tongue, teeth, throat. She choked and spat him out again, a long string of saliva connecting her lips to his cock.

"Up, up," Patrick said, winded as if he were out of breath from running. Abby had no idea what he meant at first. He tugged at her shoulders.

The elevator doors dinged open. Her heart skipped a beat when she realized what he wanted her to do. Abby straightened in an effort to hide him. She snapped her head around, startled like hell. Luckily nobody was directly outside. But she heard people around the corner.

She pressed the button for three floors up and slammed the "close door" button.

"Hold the elevator!" somebody yelled.

She rapid-fire pressed the button until the door closed and the elevator started moving again.

"Close one," she winked up at Patrick.

He stared down at her, wide-eyed and sweaty. "Holy shit," was all he could say.

She licked and sucked him a few quick times before the doors opened again. At which point she took no more chances and pulled his pants back up. Patrick took a cue, tucking in his shirt and zipping up again. Abby pressed the button for their floor. When they arrived, a man and a woman were waiting to get on.

The man only shrugged with an annoyed glance at them. The woman winked knowingly at Abby.

That feeling of power rushed over her. She waited for Patrick to take the lead. He stood, just staring at her as if she were an alien.

"Which way to your room?" Abby said.

"Oh." He pointed the wrong way first. And then he chuckled and took her by the hand to her room. "This way."

When he unlocked the room with her key and pushed her inside, it was Abby's turn to be speechless.

THE DEED

lowers of all types and colors decorated the inside of the hotel room. Mums, roses, tulips. White, red, purple, yellow. On the dresser, the bedside tables, the bed itself. The door clicked shut behind her, but Abby barely noticed. When he put his arms around her waist, she breathed in the scent of all the flowers.

"It's so beautiful," she said.

"Glad you like them," he said.

"But how... Sorry for being blunt, but this must've cost a small fortune."

"For a waiter busting his ass off?" Patrick winked at her. "I'm also really good at the blackjack table."

She thought he was simply joking with her at first. But the serious expression on his face told her otherwise.

"Blackjack paid my way through college so far," he said. "And it allows me to have my own place."

Abby kissed him on the bottom lip. "Thank you for every-thing." She frowned. "And so we're clear, you can have back what you paid me."

He cupped her face and kissed her back. "That would ruin the fun of the roleplaying."

After some kissing and groping, Abby turned to the bed.

On the bed next to the roses were piles of white rope, a box of condoms, and a black blindfold. He gently nudged her. She playfully resisted him at first, and then slowly allowed him to move her. Once at the bed, he pushed her to bend forward with ass in the air.

And then he lifted the hem of her dress. By the half chuckle, half growl he made, he must've been pleasantly surprised that she wore no panties. Patrick got down on his knees behind her and licked her. Up the insides of her thighs, to her pussy lips, the clit, a tease on the ass. He got her wet. He stripped off her dress.

And then told her to lie flat on the bed.

She did as she was told. Uncertainty flashed in her mind. What was he going to do to her? Would she like it? Patrick took her hand and smiled at her. She gave him a smile back. Screw it—whatever he did, she wanted to let him please her. Abby put her arms behind her head and spread her legs.

Patrick pushed her legs back together. He must've saw the confusion on her face. He winked, and then grabbed one of the ropes. He tied her ankles together, winding the rope up her calves and then her thighs.

"Too tight?" he said.

"Feels fine," she said.

"If you need to be freed, let me know," he said. He slipped the knot loose, to show her how fast he could undo the binding. He retied the handiwork.

And then he put a pillow underneath her head. Patrick took her hands and used another rope to bind her wrists together. Abby struggled against the restraints, testing the knots. They were solid. She had no easy way to escape, if any. Her heart raced so fast she was certain Patrick could hear it.

"Jack rabbit," she said.

Without hesitation, Patrick slipped the knots undone quickly. In fast order, Abby was released, safe. She sat up.

"You okay?" he said, laying a hand on her shoulder.

"Yeah," she said. "Maybe a drink of water?"

He hopped off the bed and opened the fridge near the bathroom sink. He got out two bottles of water, handing her one.

"We can do this without the bindings," he said. "I'd still have fun."

She took a sip of water, smiling. "I still want to be tied up. Maybe fewer ropes this time?"

"How about only the wrists?"

"Sounds good," she said. "And hey, thanks for respecting the safe word."

He smiled at her. Then he kissed her on the lips. "No problem sweet lady."

Patrick tied up her wrists like he had before. And then with a wink, he raised her arms above her head. He wrapped the other rope around her torso and criss-crossed around her breasts, pushing them up He asked if that was okay. She laughed and told him yes. The ropes rubbed her skin when she tried to move, for sure they'd leave red marks after he took them off. Abby had never imagined what it was like to wear ropes, the sensation of being confined and exposed at the same time.

It made her feel sexy. Liberated.

And then he pushed her back flat against the mattress. He slipped on a condom. And then he grabbed hold of the bindings on her wrists, raising her hands above her head. Abby closed her eyes. Little kisses down her neck and across her breasts sent shivers across her skin. She wanted to wrap her arms around his neck, and fought him to do so. But she couldn't win against the rope and his strength.

He pulled away from her, admiring the view. Abby imagined it in her own mind—her naked body, tied up, vulnerable.

And then he slipped the blindfold over her eyes. Her heart raced in anticipation and longing. She pleaded for him to do something, and when nothing happened she panicked. Was he going to do anything? He was still there, she could feel his weight shifting around on the mattress.

When he entered her, she let out a throaty moan, partly to play her part as a willing slut. Partly—mostly—because he just felt right inside her. The way he filled her and stretched her. The way he wiggled his hips, settling on top of her body. He held her close, gently, as if she were fragile.

"Is this what you paid me four-hundred dollars for?" Abby said. "To fuck me like your girlfriend?"

Patrick laughed. He pushed himself off her. And then he clutched her ankles roughly, lifting her legs over his shoulders. Abby wiggled and squirmed as if to get away. He forced himself inside her. Much less gentle than before. Still felt like him, with the familiar shape of his cock and the scent of him all over. But otherwise it could've been a different man.

One who didn't care about her pleasure. Only that she was a pussy to be taken and filled. Being used heightened the sensation for Abby in ways she hadn't expected.

He pulled out regularly, told her what a useless slut she was. How she was only good for one thing.

"Please put it back in me," Abby said, surprised at how dry and husky her voice sounded. Surprised at the words that came out of her mouth. She'd never talked like that, even to men she loved.

She just wanted it—needed it—badly.

Patrick alternated between fucking her with his cock, playing with her clit, and calling her a dirty slut. He pinched and twisted her nipples. Slapped her breasts. Flipped her over and took her from behind.

Tears welled up underneath the blindfold. Abby let out a window-shattering scream when she orgasmed.

But he kept going.

He smacked her on the ass. And man-handled her onto her back again.

She had no idea what time it was, or how long he'd been doing her, or how much longer he'd go. And then he yanked his cock out of her. She heard the snap of his condom. For a brief moment, Abby worried he'd enter her bareback and come inside her.

And then she felt the warm spray of his jizz on her stomach. On her breasts. Her neck. He just kept coming, over and over until it seemed like she was coated with him.

Patrick took off the blindfold first. She was surprised at how dark it had gotten. Then he untied her, letting her relax.

He pulled her close to him.

"I thought you going to leave?" she said, half joking and afraid he'd take her seriously.

"I'll give you another hundred bucks if you shut up and let cuddle," he said.

She obeyed, laying her head on his chest and relaxing in his arms.

Right before she fell asleep, he got out from under her and got dressed. He kissed her goodnight.

And then tossed a hundred dollar bill on the nightstand. Before she could argue with him, he left.

EPILOGUE

The next morning, Abby felt like five-hundred bucks in more ways than one. She took all the flowers with her, though she knew they wouldn't survive the trip home. She planned to dry them out and maybe save them as mementos. No way she could've left them in the hotel room.

Speeding down the highway, Abby went commando with Patrick's money stuffed in her bra. She no sign of him in the casino or hotel. Just as well.

What happened last night was fun and special in its own way. Seeing him one more time would've broken the spell.

She stopped for lunch in Iowa. While she waited for her burger, her phone buzzed with a text message.

I enjoyed myself, Patrick wrote. *Thank you.*

THANK YOU!!! she wrote back. Then she added a heart emoji.

He sent a heart back to her, and then added, *See you during your next vacation?*

You know it, Abby wrote. *Vegas next time???*

Sounds like fun!

Abby sank into the booth, content and completely happy. She didn't want to go back home. Or go back to work. She didn't even want to eat the burger when it arrived. Daydreams about Las Vegas and all the things Patrick might do filled her brain to capacity.

The next vacation couldn't come soon enough. Planning for it would the first thing she did when she got home.

ONLY A LITTLE PRACTICE

WAITING FOR HIM TO SHOW UP

Stephanie sank lower into the restaurant booth, the vinyl seat squeaking underneath her butt. Her blind date wasn't coming. At this point, she no longer cared, and that was okay.

The smells of pancakes, maple syrup, and hot apple pie made her stomach growl loud enough to be heard from the parking lot. The waitress, obviously knowing full well what the situation was, kept stopping by, asking if Stephanie might like a refill of coffee or a slice of French silk on the house. She declined both, not wanting the need to pee right as the dude (maybe) showed up, and definitely not wanting pity.

A hardcover edition of *A Tale of Two Cities* sat in front of her like a useless brick. She cracked open the cover to the first page and immediately got a reminder why she flunked out of English Lit in college.

The best of times, the worst of times, blah blah blah, who gave two shits to read the entire damn run-on sentence that never seemed to end, and right when you thought it ended, it kept going, only to make you wonder if you really needed the pie and coffee and maybe a little pity from a waitress...

The book was meant for Tom, so he could recognize her. He'd have a purple carnation for her—Stephanie insisted on that rather than a red freaking rose.

Romance? Who needed romance? Mostly, she just hoped to get laid. Short of that, a free pie would hit the spot.

Even if the waitress was the one offering. The pie, of course.

Stephanie sighed, waving the waitress over. She took another coffee and the French silk.

And to think, she wore her favorite blue dress, with the scoop low enough to show off what little cleavage Stephanie had, and short enough to feel like a tease without giving away too many goods. She wore a pair of white high heel sandals, a silver pentagram around her neck, and tiny silver earrings.

All that dressing up, to impress the waitress enough to feel sorry for her.

Stephanie never should've let Mary talk her into this blind date. She told Mary how much she hated these things, how stressful they were, how damn awkward.

What was more awkward, though, was telling Mary that her cousin could stay home and forget about it.

Because at the end of it, there was that small chance of ending the night in bed with a handsome man. And no matter how small the chance might be, it beat staying at home in her pajamas binge watching Netflix.

Stephanie checked her watch. Thirty minutes of no show. How long was too long? She wished she knew. Out of practice was too kind.

She tossed her shoulder length brown hair, then whistled quietly to herself. The pie finally came and not a moment too soon. The waitress topped off her coffee with a kind smile she could've kept to herself, and patted her on the shoulder before walking off to the next table.

In a weird way, Stephanie wished the waitress had sat down with her, a habit of family diner waitresses everywhere that she found annoying. Charles Dickens certainly didn't turn out to be great company. On the next blind date, Stephanie was bringing some old school science fiction. If a man can't appreciate Ben Bova or Andre Norton, he wasn't worth dating. Or sleeping with for that matter.

She lifted her fork and stabbed the end of her pie.

"So sorry I'm late."

Stephanie heard the words, recognized what they meant, yet didn't comprehend who they were meant for.

And then she made eye contact with the most handsome man she'd met in far too long. Easy brown eyes, brownish red hair parted down one side and slicked back, and the cutest dimples. He wore a green dress shirt with the sleeves rolled up, black jeans, and shiny black dress shoes. He looked intellectual, and had an artist's flair.

"Hi," Stephanie said. She barely moved, like a rabbit in a garden staring at a predator and hoping like hell he'd just go away. Her fork remained in the pie.

He set a purple carnation on top of the book. "I'm Tom."

Before things turned any more deadly serious awkward, she introduced herself. Thankfully, Tom didn't offer to shake her hand or pat her on the shoulder. He simply sat across from her.

"How's the pie here?" he said.

"Okay," she said. "Good, I hear. I don't know really."

He pointed at the French silk pie. "Well, as soon as you find out, let me know. That one looks delicious."

The waitress walked by casually, as if nothing were amiss. Tom ordered coffee with cream and the same pie as Stephanie. She winked at Stephanie and gave her a thumbs up behind Tom's back.

"So how do you know my cousin?" he asked.

"Who's your cousin," she said. "Oh, right."

"Mary," he said slowly, as if guessing at the correct answer for Trivial Pursuit.

"Yeah," she said. "I knew her in college. Still know her, as a matter of fact. You know what? I want to start over."

"We just started," he said. "If this doesn't feel right for you, I can go."

Stephanie placed her hand on his wrist.

"No stay," she said. Then she realized how clingy that felt, and let his wrist go. "I'm just not very good at this, I guess."

"I'm not either," he said.

"You're doing fine," she said.

"You'll find this hard to believe," he said. "But I have a secret for you."

"Oh?"

"Come here closer," he wiggled his finger in a come hither motion. She leaned forward. "You're doing fine, too."

Stephanie laughed. Exhaling all that excess air into a chuckle felt good, actually. So she let loose and kept laughing, which made him laugh too. No words really necessary. He had a wonderful, easy laugh that made dimples in his cheeks.

She finally ate a bite of her pie. The chocolate tasted smooth and wonderful and mixed well with the bitter coffee already staining her tongue.

They small talked for some time. What do you do? How long have you lived here? Any pets?

Turned out, Tom was a professional artist—a graphic designer with a side gig as a high school art teacher. He'd lived in town since he graduated with a masters in business. And he had a pet hamster. Far more interesting than a dental hygienist wanting to go back to school with no pets—also known as Stephanie's current lot in life.

"You're far more interesting than I was afraid of," he said. "Sorry that came out wrong."

She patted him on the hand. "I'm not interesting at all."

"Excuse me?" he said. "Art history major? And a fascination with the High Medieval era? Come on, how many chicks do you think I've met like you?"

"We grow on trees," Stephanie said.

Tom laughed. And then he ate one more bite of his pie, and shoved the plate towards her. She finished off the last bite for him.

"I wish I'd chosen the more practical sensible route like you," she said. "Becoming a professional tooth brusher wasn't the first choice, of course. But I could've chosen something with more of a future."

"Business wasn't what I wanted to do," he said. "Though I admit it's opened a few more doors than studying art."

"Yeah, I'm sure," she said. "Not all of us can make a living at teaching or making art."

"But you can still practice," he said.

"That's why I keep a sketch book." Stephanie opened her mouth, then hesitated before saying the next thought in her brain. Then, fuck it, life was too short. "Come over to my place some time, and I'd love to show you."

"I'd like that," Tom said.

Tonight? She wanted to ask him, but couldn't quite make that one little word go from her brain to her lips. In the blink of her eyes, she saw the rest of the night in a mini-movie— they'd pour over her sketch books, he'd tell her how talented and beautiful she was, then she'd kiss him. And then later in her bedroom...

"You okay?" he said.

"Huh?" she said. "Yeah. Just being a space cadet, sorry."

Tom held her hand. She hadn't even noticed until she did. It just felt right. His warm hand enveloped hers. She placed her hand on top of his and smiled.

"I think they want to close the restaurant," he said. "You have any other plans for tonight?"

"No, nowhere else to be," she said.

The waitress gave Stephanie another thumbs up. She tried to ignore her. A blush heated up Stephanie's neck and cheeks.

"This was a wonderful night," Tom said. "Thank you. Just wish it could go on a little longer."

"Thank you, sir," she said. She briefly told herself *no* to what she was about to do. But then she did it anyways. "I have Netflix."

"Sounds like a wonderful way to end the night," he said. "And if it still doesn't end, I bought condoms earlier. Unless that's too presumptuous."

"Perhaps a little," Stephanie said. "But we're on the same page."

The waitress squealed. Tom turned around to see what the fuss was about. He laughed, raising one eyebrow in mock amazement.

"Perhaps we should leave for our own safety," he said.

Stephanie snorted. "She's been cheering me on all night," she said.

"Meet you at your place?" he stood up and then kissed her on the lips.

"I'll text the directions," she said.

Her fingers shook as she typed and then retyped the directions. And then she couldn't leave the restaurant and dig her car keys out of her purse fast enough.

AND THEN FIGURING OUT WHAT TO DO

For a few minutes, Stephanie worried that Tom chickened out on her. Just her luck to score a fun night with a sexy man and come up empty handed.

But then her doorbell rang. Tom stood on her front porch with a red rose in one hand and a plastic bag in the other. She let him. Tom handed her the rose and left the plastic bag on the table in the front hall. Stephanie peeked inside to find the aforementioned box of condoms. She smiled to herself.

And then she led him to the living room. Stephanie sniffed the rose, and placed it on the coffee table. He picked up the blanket and spread it wide while she turned on the TV.

"Want popcorn?" she said. "Or anything to drink?"

"I'm okay if you are," Tom said.

She was perfectly fine. Mostly, she wanted to just be close to him. And get on with the fun part of the night.

"Now the big question," she said, turning on Netflix. "What to watch?"

"I'm open to about anything," he said. "I'm partial to science fiction."

"Star Trek?" she said.

"I've meant to watch Deep Space Nine lately."

A man after her own heart. She found the show and started up the pilot episode. While the opening credits rolled, Stephanie cuddled close to Tom under the blanket. He wrapped his arm around her shoulders. Her elbow ended up on his upper thigh, near his crotch. So close, she imagined feeling him getting hard.

They chatted a little during the show. Small talk, poking fun at the cheesiness of the pilot episode, reminiscing over the good times that were the 1990s.

Meanwhile, his fingers massaged her upper arm. And then wandered ever closer to touching her on the breast. Near the end of the episode, right as the climax happened, he cupped her and squeezed gently. Stephanie had her fingers up her dress, rubbing at her panties.

She got wet from the lazy masturbation. Her elbow slid further up his thigh, right against the stiff teepee in his jeans.

Stephanie didn't think she could last another episode, as much as she enjoyed Star Trek. But she let the next episode autoplay.

Luckily, Tom seemed to have the same idea she had.

With one finger on her chin, he nudged her to face him. Then he kissed her.

Once the kiss ended, she touched him on the chest. "You sure about this?"

"Yes," he said.

"We'll be more comfortable in the bedroom," she said.

Tom kissed her once more, her lips pleasantly swollen already, and then he threw the blanket off of them. He glanced quickly down her body, at her dress rumpled around her waist, the hint of black panties, and then back up to her eyes.

He scooped her up into his arms. Not exactly smooth, but

he did his best. Stephanie helped him out with positioning. Finally he stood and lifted her.

When he walked by the front table, Stephanie reached out and grabbed the plastic bag with the condoms.

"Upstairs?" he said.

"Yup," she said. "First door on the left."

His strong arms held her steady all the way up. She kissed and nibbled at his neck.

Luckily, Stephanie left her bedside light on before heading out. Tom tossed her onto the queen sized bed like a sack of grain. He took the bag and set it aside next to her clock radio.

And then he got down on his knees in front of her. Stephanie held up a finger.

"Hold that thought for a sec." She maneuvered around the bed, tossed the decorative pillows off to one side, and pulled the comforter down and tossed it to the floor too. "Okay, ready."

She spread her legs wide, placing her ankles over his shoulders. His face was right in front of her pussy. He could've reached out with his tongue and tasted her panties.

But he ignored her pussy.

Instead, Tom kissed the edge of her panty-line. He ran his lips and tongue down the inside of her left thigh. Then up her right thigh. He massaged her leg muscles with his fingers. Then slowly kissed down to her knee, her calves, keeping eye contact with her the entire time.

Stephanie combed her fingers through his hair, messing up every strand.

And then he finally kissed her right between the legs. She closed her thighs together out of reflex, trapping his head in place. She giggled. He forced her legs back wide open. Tom pressed his lips against her panties, flicking his tongue against her labia through the thin fabric.

Stephanie covered her face with her arms. She closed her eyes, content to simply feel what he was doing. His warm fingers pulling aside her panties, poking her, rubbing and licking.

Finally, once her panties had a warm wet spot, he took them off. He rolled his tongue across her labia and up her hood. Then down to her anus and back up. He teased her, toying with her.

And then he slid a finger inside her. Slowly finger fucked her. In, back out, in. He varied his rhythm, focused with his tongue for a bit, then his finger, then added another finger.

He curled his fingers inside her, touching and stroking her G-spot. She squeezed her legs shut again. Or at least tried to. He kept a firm hand on one of her thighs while doing his magic with the other.

An orgasm warmed her from the belly and radiated out. Her skin itched with heat. The world shrank down to only her, him, and the bed underneath. Stephanie curled her toes.

And then she screamed.

She scooted away from him before the flood came. The orgasm kept rocking her body. She rolled her eyes up, covered her mouth, and let out another scream.

When she came down from the high, Tom was staring at her with a satisfied grin on his face.

"You're not done with me," she ordered.

"Nope," he said. Tom took off his shirt, nearly popping off the buttons. He made a move to continue his ravaging.

But Stephanie stopped him with a raised finger.

"First," she said. "I need to return the favor."

The grin on his face widened, showing off his dimples. Tom loosened his belt buckle. When he didn't go fast enough for Stephanie, she helped him the rest of the way out of his jeans. He took the liberty of unzipping and sliding her dress off her shoulders.

She made him lay flat on his back. Tom put his arms under his head. Then she stripped off his boxer briefs, revealing a wonderful half-erect cock with a trimmed patch of fur above it.

Stephanie stroked him from base to tip, taking her time just as he did with her. On the way down, she fondled his balls gently, barely touching. He still reacted, shifting his weight as if trying to get away from her.

And then she took him into her mouth a little bit at a time. Only a taste. His salty precum coated her tongue. She swallowed him further, taking him as far as she could go. It'd been awhile since she tried this...

Breathing through her nose, she deep throated him all the way, balls deep.

"Oh my god yeah," he said.

She held him in her throat for a moment. And then spat him back out. A thick string of saliva connected her mouth to his shaft.

"Liked that?" she said.

"Yes," he said. "Thank you."

He pushed her head back down onto him. He didn't force her to go all the way again. But she still had to catch her breath fast.

She slowly licked and teased him with her teeth. He played with her hair, moaning and quietly encouraging her on.

And then she sped up her pace. Frantic. Like she wanted, needed his come. Then slowed down again. She varied the pace, making him guess what she was going to do next.

"Okay, stop," he said. "I need to be inside you soon."

"Soon?" she said. "How about when I say so."

He laughed, clearly taken back by her sudden dominance. If he didn't enjoy it, he kept that to himself. Tom held his cock in one hand, as if to offer it to her, for her pleasure.

Stephanie rolled her tongue across his tip.

He begged her with his eyes. The room smelled of cock, wet pussy, and sweat. She couldn't say no to him much longer.

She held him by the cock, and straddled on top of him. Kissing him up the stomach and then chest, up his neck, she sat on top of him.

She reached over to the box of condoms. She got one out, opened the package, and slipped it over him.

And then took him inside her. She wiggled her hips around, feeling him rub against her G-spot in just the right way.

Tom massaged her breasts, pinching the nipples and licking them when she bent over him close enough.

And then she got a kinky idea out of nowhere.

She stopped screwing him. He must've thought she was teasing him, because he slapped her on the backside.

"I have an idea," she touched him on the chest. "Just having second thoughts."

"Tell me your idea," he said. "We'll decide together if we want to do it."

"Okay," she said. "We just had a blind date."

"Right," he said.

Stephanie rolled off of him and opened her bedside table. What she was looking for happened to be right on top.

Her blindfold. She got it as a Christmas gift one year, used it once, and hadn't cared for it.

Tom chuckled. "I see where this is going."

"Do you?" Stephanie chuckled.

He leaned up on his elbow. "Is that for me? Or for you?"

"I was thinking for me."

"Okay, so..." he said. "Let's say if I put the blindfold on you, I can't hold onto your hands or wrists. And I can't tie you down. That way you can take the blindfold off any time."

"Sounds good," she handed him the blindfold. Her heart beat rapidly. She had no idea what she'd just agreed to do. And that excited her more than she thought it would.

And then she turned around. He slipped the blindfold over her head and adjusted it over her eyes.

"Can you see anything?" he asked.

"Nope," she said.

And then he pressed her forward between her shoulders, putting her in a doggy pose. Stephanie tried to breath normal. But that was hard. For a long time, he didn't do anything.

Then she felt something. His finger? Yes... Just lightly touching her, stroking her labia and clit, probing. And then felt something else that definitely wasn't his finger. This felt like latex and slightly wet.

He slid his cock into her.

"Talk dirty to me," she said.

"You dirty whore," he said. "You like being fucked like this?"

"Yes. Just like that."

He grabbed her by the hips. "Little slut. Giving up the goods on the first date."

"Yes."

Tom took her by the hair and pulled. "You like being taken advantage of by a stranger?"

"Oh god, yeah." Her pussy became soaking wet. Between his needy thrusting and dirty words, Stephanie was about to lose her mind. Not being able to see him, see what he was doing to her, made it all the more exciting.

"Good whore," he said. Tom slapped her on the ass. Hard. She kept feeling the slap long after he did it, his hand print burning her skin. Her entire body burned with need.

"I'm a good whore," she said. "And I'm all yours."

Stephanie never would've imagined herself saying such

vile words, not even in her fantasies. But here she was, saying them. Maybe she'd regret them in the morning.

But for now, her world was pure blackness, and the only things that mattered were what she could feel and smell.

She felt his cock ramming her faster and faster. And she smelled her own pussy dripping.

And then she exploded in orgasm. Another followed right after. And another...

Tom stopped fucking her. But he kept his cock inside. She came on him, squirting all over him.

He pulled out of her. She wanted to roll over and relax, take off the blindfold and cuddle in his arms. But Tom held her by the hair.

And then she felt a series of searing hot drops on her backside. He came on her. She never thought he'd stop. Surely, he covered her back with his come.

Finally he let her go. Stephanie relaxed on her stomach, out of breath and completely spent. Tom stripped the blindfold off her eyes. Truth was, she'd forgotten about it.

He gave her a pillow, and placed another pillow by her. He settled down next to her, one arm holding her close. Stephanie snuggled next to him, smearing both of their juices together.

She tried chatting with him, but he was drifting off to sleep pretty fast.

But as far as blind dates went, this one ended pretty damn good.

Even in a literal sense.

PRACTICING MAKES EVERYTHING BETTER

The next week, Stephanie sat across from Tom at another restaurant. She couldn't go back to the other one, with the waitress who almost certainly knew what had happened. Not like it should matter.

She held his hand. He rolled his thumb across her knuckles. They both ate French silk and had coffee.

"This is getting to be a habit," he said.

Stephanie shrugged. She wore a different dress this time —shorter, black, and with her boobs pressed higher up. And she wore black over-the-knee boots. Not like she was telling him outright what she wanted or anything.

"How is it a habit?" she said, winking at him. "Habits require repetition to become habit. Don't you know?"

"No, I guess not," he said. "Repetition sounds bad though."

"It does, doesn't it."

"Think we can use practice to build a habit?" he said.

She thought about that for a moment. Practice sounded far more fun than repetition.

"I like that," she said.

He stacked his pie plate on top of hers and shoved them both aside.

"One problem," he said. "This isn't a blind date anymore."

"What's wrong with having a second blind date?" she winked.

"That sounds like fun," he said.

Stephanie paid the bill.

And then later when she brought him home, she blindfolded him.

THE BEST NON-DATE EVER

IN WHICH MARISSA DUMPS ONE DATE

arissa stole a glance at the stranger who'd been eyeballing her all night. Tall, shaggy brown hair, an easy going smile with dimples. He wore a tuxedo well, the cummerbund even turned right-side up and the bowtie on straight. Certainly James Bond type, not suave enough, but good looking.

Unfortunately, he wasn't her date.

Not like Marissa got invited to a fancy charity dinner at an art exhibition show every week. The crab was to die for, as were the little green beans and the biscuits served with the meal. If Marissa hadn't been so worried about how she fit into her glitzy purple evening gown, she might've snatched another biscuit or two to go with her Cabernet.

Her date—Gerald Oxingham III—was a rich ass-creep, though at least a reasonably good looking one. As the night progressed, attractive turned into good looking to only reasonably so.

And she wasn't even sure about that anymore.

Could she score with him after the party? Sure. Would she feel good about herself after? Hell, no.

He schmoozed with the richest of the rich people, including and especially all the rich wives and girlfriends. He played drinking games with the obnoxious younger men, and bragged of tall tales about sexual conquest around the older men. Gerald was the eminent wannabe with too much money and not enough common sense.

So Marissa strolled among the paintings and sculptures that were to be auctioned later in the evening. She loved the abstracts. She adored the post modern. But she spent most of her time around all the nudes.

Male or female didn't matter, bodies fascinated her. The gentle curve of a woman that resembled hills and dunes. The way a man's bare and muscular thigh led the eye upward. Even better, the intertwining of the two during love making.

Once, Marissa modeled nude for her own sugar daddy, a playboy artist who had a studio on his own vineyard. He never painted his models' faces—he always found a way to cover the face with hair or vegetation. He always made Marissa feel beautiful. Helped that he pretty much paid for her college education.

Not like she'd ever tell her parents that.

"Hello," somebody said next to her.

Marissa turned away from the painting she was looking at. The man with shaggy brown hair stood only a few feet away. Up close he seemed even more handsome. His green eyes glinted with a touch of humor and more than a little curiosity.

"Hi there," she said. Marissa introduced herself.

"Ethan," he said.

"Are you an artist?" she said.

"Reporter, actually," he said. "They still made me wear this penguin suit."

Marissa touched him on the arm. "You look great in it."

"You're too kind," he said.

She smiled up at him. The silence lasted longer than she expected. She figured he'd wish her a good night and wander off. He kept staring down at his shiny black dress shoes, as if uncertain of what to say.

"You know what would make this more interesting?" she said.

"What's that?"

"The party," she said. "You know what might make the party more interesting?"

He held a finger up to his chin as if deep in thought. "Clearly, you mean they should serve more of those biscuits."

"I know right!" she said. Her stomach rumbled a little. Marissa hoped like hell he didn't hear that. "But I was thinking, I'd have more fun with a proper date."

Ethan took a step back. Marissa felt bad, and knew that had been the wrong thing to say. But he still played it cool.

"I'm sorry to hear that," he said, and he actually did sound sorry for her. Ethan glanced in the direction where Gerald was kissing ass with some CEO looking guys. "Is that him?"

"Yup," Marissa said. "The world's most interesting non-date."

He rubbed his neck, pretending to look at the nude painting in front of them, which featured a man with a giant cock standing in a field of wild flowers. Marissa could've sworn she saw that exact image, slightly altered, on a steamy romance cover once or twice. She doubted Ethan was appreciating the painting in the same way she was.

"He is a giant among men," he said. "The guy in the painting, not your date."

Marissa smiled and touched him on the arm. "Really? I only noticed the background of wild flowers."

"Seriously?" he said. Then he laughed when he figured out she was being sarcastic. "I'm a dork."

She smacked him gently on the shoulder. Why couldn't

she have scored a date with Ethan, instead of Gerald? She always attracted the guys who only wanted to score. Guys like Ethan were nice to her, but never took a chance and asked one simple question.

"Do you know if the auction starts any time soon?" he said.

That wasn't the question Marissa had in mind. "I think it's scheduled for closer to midnight. I might be asleep by then."

He nodded. "That's the only thing the newspaper sent me here for."

"The auction?" she said.

"Well, one painting in particular," Ethan said. Then he pointed at the painting of the man with the giant cock.

"Wait? Seriously?" she said. "What's so special about this?"

"It appeared on several romance book covers apparently," he said. "Seems it caused a scandal."

"Hold on a minute." Marissa stepped closer to the painting and squinted at the bottom left corner. There it was —a familiar chicken-scratch signature, Harold Patroklus. The artist who paid for her college education. "Holy shit."

"Yeah, no kidding," Ethan said.

"No... I knew the artist," she said. "I... uh... posed for him. Didn't realize he painted men too."

"Oh," he said. Ethan studied her, his eyes roaming up and down her body.

Marissa regretted telling him that little piece of her history. Just like her to trust the innocent nice guy with that. Not like it mattered. What did she expect anyway?

He opened his mouth. Then closed it.

"What?" Marissa said, crossing her arms over her chest.

"Nothing," he said.

"Just say whatever you want to say." She heard the defensive tone in her voice, and hated it. Whatever chances she had with this guy, no matter how imperfect he was, she dashed.

"Just wanted to say that you're beautiful," he said. "And that your nudes would definitely fetch more money on auction than this hunk of cheese." He pointed at the big cock painting.

Marissa laughed, despite herself. "Thanks."

"I didn't want to offend you," he said.

"You didn't," she held her hands out in surrender. "I guess it's a sore spot for me."

"Why?" The question, and the way Ethan asked it, seemed serious enough. He didn't smile, or wink. He only asked a legitimate question.

A tough question, though.

"I did it because the money was good," she said. Marissa waved a hand as if swatting a fly. "No, that's not entirely right. Yes, the money. But the money bought me freedom from my parents. I didn't have to wait for my dumb high school boyfriend to propose. I packed up and moved to college instead."

"Because of your modeling?" he said.

"Yup. In a way, Harold took care of me. He never took me in, or fed me directly, never asked for anything. Always professional. He made posing a positive experience."

"Glad to hear that," Ethan said.

"I don't know," she said. "Not everyone saw the positive. The fun. The stupid boyfriend didn't approve. I assume my parents wouldn't have either."

"And who are they to judge you for doing something fun?" he said.

This time, Marissa opened her mouth and closed it. She wasn't sure how to answer that. All her adult life, she figured they—boyfriends, parents, room mates—had judged her for posing nude. Not once had someone asked her such a simple question as Ethan just asked.

Who were they anyway?

Ethan shrugged. "Just saying. If they loved you, they'd see the positive too."

Marissa sighed. "But, how could they? I was their little girl. Or the girlfriend-maybe-wife one day."

"You know I'm right," he said, matter of factly.

"Yeah, I do." She touched him on the shoulder. "Thanks."

When her hand fell off his shoulder, he reached for her fingers. And then gave them a quick squeeze.

"I enjoyed talking to you," he said.

And like that, he turned and wished her good night. Just like that, he'd step out of her life. Somebody who connected with her, understood her even if for only a brief moment.

"Wait," said Marissa. "Can I get you a drink?"

He turned back to face her. And smiled, showing off his cute dimples. "I noticed the terrace is mostly empty. And has a lovely view of the city."

"I'll bring the drinks out," she said. "What's your poison?"

"Cabernet," he said.

She smiled and promised to see him in a few minutes. They went in opposite directions.

And just like that, Marissa had a new date for the night.

IN WHICH MARISSA HOOKS UP
WITH ANOTHER DATE

She had no trouble avoiding Gerald as she snagged two glasses of red wine and a small plate of chocolate truffles. Marissa slipped out to the terrace. Through the sycamore trees and down the bluffs, the city lights glowed like stars below her. The breeze was gentle on her arms, barely stroking her hair. She set the treats down on a wooden bench in a darker, more private part of the terrace, behind a garden of rose bushes.

Marissa waited. Unsure if Ethan would show up, she closed her eyes and just tried to breath normally. Wouldn't be the first time a man had chickened out on her after promising to meet her.

About to give up, she stood. And then Ethan showed up with another plate of chocolate truffles. His bowtie was undone, and he'd ditched the cummerbund. He looked more handsome that way, like he didn't care if he was properly put together.

"Looks like we had the same idea," he said.

Marissa tapped her temple. "Great minds, thinking alike."

She sat back down on the bench. He sat next to her,

handing over his plate of truffles. She gave him a glass of wine. After clinking glasses, they shared the two plates of snacks.

"Beautiful night," she said, completely and utterly unsure of what to say. Had she really asked him to come out here? When was the last time she'd done something like that? A very long time ago, if ever.

"Quite beautiful," Ethan said. "Always loved the view from up here."

"Not your first time taking a girl out here?" she said.

"Sorry, you're not the first." He chuckled, rubbing his hands on his pants. "Probably not the last, unless you convince me otherwise."

Marissa swatted him on the knee. "Oh? What would it take to convince you to stop inviting girls to a secret rendezvous?"

He shrugged one shoulder, as if unsure how to answer that. Instead of answering, he scooted closer to her. His body heat warmed her. Marissa smiled prettily, not content to let him have an easy win.

"Might take some convincing," he said. "No lady has persuaded me yet."

She sipped her wine, staring at him with one eye half closed. "I'm not sure what you mean."

"I mean to say," he said, leaning towards her just a little bit, "is how do I kiss you?"

She leaned towards him. "With your lips."

Ethan brushed his lips against hers. Just a light kiss, and it was over before she realized what exactly just happened.

And then he picked up a truffle, and offered it to her. He fed her.

"To be honest," he said. "You're only the second girl. Not sure if that destroys whatever fantasy you have of me."

"Only the second?" She offered him a truffle, and fed him.

"Not like I get invited to fancy parties every week," he said.

Marissa laughed at that. "Neither do I, my friend."

"Full disclosure," he said. "I'm here to write an article about your date."

"Oh? I'm surprised he doesn't lick up the attention." She sipped at her wine, alcohol getting to her head rather quickly. Or maybe that was something else.

"The editor at the newspaper thought the same as you do," he said. "Thing is, Gerald doesn't want to talk to you if you don't have a pussy, or aren't a frat boy."

Marissa laughed a little too loud, her giggle echoing among the trees. "Now that you say it like that, yeah, that sounds like Gerald."

"I got a little out of him," Ethan said. "Not much. I might have to make up a story, or something. Or write about other people more than Gerald."

"Which he won't appreciate," she said. "The man is an attention whore."

"I've heard him called worse things."

"It's alright," she said. "you don't have to apologize for him. He is what he is."

"So I've been told."

"He isn't all bad."

"Must've been some reason for you to go out with him." Ethan said that without any hint of sarcasm or malice. Marissa appreciated that. Nice to know Ethan was different from Gerald. That Ethan wasn't trying to be competitive and get in a pissing match with Gerald.

"I heard he's well endowed." Marissa left the double meaning unexplained. Of course, she meant endowed by the inheritance he got from his father. The money inheritance.

"That's what the newspaper article was to be about,"

Ethan said with a wry grin. He left the double meaning hanging too.

Marissa raised her eyebrows. She scooted closer to him, their thighs touching. "He does like to use his endowment. Sometimes for the better, though I've had some disagreements over how he should use it."

"How so?" Ethan said, concern on his face. "I'll report you as an anonymous source in the article."

"Thank you," she said. She cleared her throat. "It's all in how he uses his big endowment to get what he wants."

"How so?" Ethan said.

"Well, Gerald has great vision. He sees the best in people, I think. But when he sticks his endowment in places where it isn't necessarily wanted, things get ugly."

"Real ugly?" he said.

"So I've heard," she said. "But I haven't seen it first hand yet."

"You wanted to see it first hand? Didn't you?" He held out his hand as if gripping something big.

Marissa sighed. "Well, yes. For awhile at least. Not so much anymore, now that I've gotten to know Gerald a little."

"Just a little?"

She pressed her thumb and forefinger together to represent the minuteness. "Tiny. Teeny tiny in ways you can't imagine."

"So you haven't actually seen it, but you have knowledge of his endowment."

"Oh heck. You know how girls talk to one another. I heard all about the endowment, and then I got shown the photos."

"Oh no. The photos?"

"The photos." Marissa wrapped her arm in Ethan's arm. "You have no idea. It's like Gerald is so proud of what little he has, that he has to share it with everyone."

"But not with you so far?" he asked. He was merciless, even if a bit redundant. Probably made him a good reporter, lining up all the facts and double checking.

"Well, give the man some credit for decency," she said. "He hasn't yet shown me the full extent of his endowment with a selfie. The photos I saw were all in texts to other girls."

The expression on Ethan's face turned serious. "I understand, through other sources, that his endowment got him in trouble with the law? Can you say substantiate that claim?"

"I don't know. I think it was common knowledge he was in jail. But not for what."

"Even those of us in the news business know exactly what happened there."

She laughed, placing a hand on his chest. Of course she knew a little about his public exposure scandal. When pressed, Gerald explained it as a prank gone wrong. Marissa hadn't entirely believed him.

"Oh?" she said. "Maybe I haven't paid attention to the news lately."

"You should," Ethan said. "Might save you from a bad date."

"Have you been in the news?" she said.

"I write the news," he said. "And I thought I was the one asking questions."

"But if you asked all the questions," she said, "wouldn't that be a little one-sided?"

"Yes," he said. "No. What?"

"How much of an endowment do you have?" she said.

He almost had a snappy response. But he shut his mouth in a tight thin line. He blushed from forehead to neck. Marissa swallowed the rest of her wine and set the glass aside.

She placed her hand high up his leg. He grew hard, tugging the fabric.

"I don't need a man with a big endowment," she said. "He just needs to know what to do with it."

Ethan took her hand before she could do anything else naughty. It wasn't the wine in her head after all. She wasn't drunk. Just happy and giddy. Marissa leaned close to him, inside his arm, nearly brushing lips again with him.

"You sure about this?" he said.

"I need this," she said.

Ethan pushed her away. She thought he decided against having fun with her. And then he unzipped his trousers. With some fumbling to get his tux shirt untucked and out of the way, he revealed his tight boxer briefs.

With an amazing bulge in the middle.

And then he slipped his boxers down. His cock sprang out. She understood why he didn't brag about his endowment right away.

She wouldn't have believed him.

He was bigger than average, bigger than any guy she'd ever been with. Porn star size, eight or nine inches for sure, with a set of heavy balls underneath. A trimmed patch of hair was above his cock, but otherwise he was smooth.

"Is this what you needed?" Ethan said.

"Oh yes," she said.

"You know why I like this spot?" he said.

"Why?"

Ethan pointed behind the bushes. "Because there's a hidden staircase back there. Goes down to the swimming pool, but along the way are nice places to be private with someone."

"I see now," Marissa said. She grabbed him by the cock, and stood up. "Want to show me?"

He stood with her, holding on to his pants while he showed her the secret trail. Sure enough it was there, just as he said.

"I brought a condom," he said. "Just in case I met someone special."

"And I'm special?" she said.

"If Gerald only realized how special," he said.

She didn't even want to think about him. If only Gerald realized how damn lucky Ethan was. Marissa led him by the cock down the stairs.

At a bend in the stairs, he pulled her aside into a little cove partially covered by hedge bushes. Inside the hedge was a wooden bench long enough for somebody to lie down on.

"Oh my," she said. This was a perfect little place to hide, as long as nobody else had the same idea.

Marissa was willing to bet they'd be safe. At least long enough to have some fun with Ethan.

IN WHICH MARISSA ENJOYS HERSELF

$\mathcal{E}$than gently nudged her to sit down on the bench. She was ready to take his cock and slowly pleasure him. But that wasn't what he had in mind apparently.

He let his trousers drop down around his ankles. And then he squatted down in front of her. Ethan lifted the hem of her dress up around her knees, pushing the glittery fabric further up. He kissed her knees, up along the insides of her thighs, teasing her with his tongue and lips.

Marissa stroked her fingers through his hair, messing it up as best she could. She spread her legs wider for him. He touched her panties with one finger, and then went back to teasing her thighs with his kisses, his fingers now finding her hips and massaging her skin.

And then he tugged on her panties. When she didn't help him out, he tugged harder, almost tearing the fragile fabric. Marissa lifted up so he could pull her panties down. She was glad she made the time to trim up her pubic hair the night before, on the off chance she'd get lucky.

She had just imagined getting lucky with her date, not a random stranger she met at the party instead.

Ethan flicked his tongue across her labia. Then he slowly stroked her with his fingers, trading off with his tongue and fingers, varying the sensations and rhythm. Marissa closed her eyes, leaned her head back, and pressed her own fingers against her clit. She rubbed herself, only somewhat aware she was doing it at all.

When she opened her eyes again, his fingers stopped doing anything at all. He backed off, simply watching, observing her masturbate.

And then he joined her masturbation, slowly stroking his long cock from tip to base. He took his time, as if mesmerized by what she was doing to herself. Together, they pleasured themselves, getting off with only eye contact and their own heavy breathing. Her bare arms felt hot, and her dress clung to her sweaty skin.

Marissa dipped her middle finger inside. She'd made out at parties, even let a boy slip a hand up her dress once. But she'd never gone this far. Never masturbated with someone. Granted, Marissa was used to tame parties. The kind of party she thought she was going to tonight.

How pleasantly wrong she was.

The fact that she could be caught at any moment kept her on edge, in a strange grey area of enjoying herself while being slightly scared of what might happen next. The fear added to sensations, building them up. In the back of her mind, she realized she wasn't truly scared at all.

Nervous perhaps. Anxious, but in a good and exciting way.

Ethan shrugged out of his jacket. Then he took off his shoes and pants. Marissa helped him with the buttons on his shirt. And he was naked in front of her. If anybody should be nervous, it should've been him. After all, she could simply close her legs and nobody would notice the difference. He was completely naked in the moonlight.

Marissa gripped his cock and brought him closer to her. She needed both hands, and still the tip poked out. He had a fat mushroom shaped head, thick veins down the shaft, and already had precum. She stroked him with her fingers and palms, not quite feeling like she could pleasure him because he was so big. Most guys, she could touch and they'd blow a load before she was ready.

Ethan just smiled down at her, stroking her hair back and telling her how good what she did felt.

"It's so big," she said. Words she never truly expected to say, yet here she was, saying them. "I'm not sure what to do."

"You're doing great," he said. "Do what feels fun for you."

"But what if it's not fun for you?" Marissa felt silly asking that, as if she were a virgin again and completely unsure of herself. She left behind her virginity long ago. Problem was, she was unsure.

"Ever sucked a cock before?" he said.

"Yes," she said. "But never one this big."

He smiled a little, trying to hide his pride at what she was telling him. "I'm no different than any other guy. Mine works the same way."

"So if I do this..." Marissa wrapped her lips around his tip and rolled her tongue across him. She made wet sloppy noises. "That feels good?"

"Oh hell yes," he said.

"And if I do this..." She lifted his heavy cock. Standing upright, he was taller than her face. She let him rest on her forehead, between her eyes, and licked and sucked one ball then the other. "Good? Yes?"

"I wish you wouldn't stop," he said.

"Like this?" Marissa touched the tip of her tongue to the base of his cock, licking upwards until she could barely reach any further, and arched her back and tilted her head up to reach the precum at his tip.

"Hmm," he moaned.

Marissa alternately licked and stroked him all over. Slowly massaging him harder, she rolled her tongue and fingers across his balls. She tried to take him into her mouth, but he was too damn big. Ethan didn't force himself on her. He let her do the work, only occasionally stroking her hair and massaging her shoulders.

He slipped one of the straps of her dress down her arm. And then the other. Then he lifted the straps back in place. She went down on him with more fury. If he blew his load all over her face, she'd consider it a night well spent.

But he persistently didn't come, no matter how much pressure she used, no matter how fast she stroked him.

"I want you inside me," she said. Even as she told him that, Marissa wasn't entirely certain she could take him. But she wanted to try.

Ethan picked up his jacket and fished the condom out of the pocket. He tore open the packet. The smell of latex and lube covered the smell of their oral sex. He slipped the condom on. Waiting, Marissa slowly rubbed her clit, making it wet.

Wetter than it already was.

"On top or bottom?" he said.

She thought about that for a moment. "Top."

Marissa wanted to control how much of that big cock went inside her. She trusted Ethan to be gentle. But she still wanted the control. Being in charge thrilled her.

Ethan sat down on the bench, and she stood up. He laid flat with his arms underneath his head, stretched out like he was at home in his own bed.

Hands on his chest, she straddled him. She kissed him on the mouth. Then gave him littles kisses down his neck and shoulder. Ethan massaged her back, finding the zipper on the back of her dress with ease. With a slow zip, he exposed her back.

Her dress slipped off her shoulders. She sat upright and wiggled out of it. Then tossed it on top of his tuxedo.

Ethan placed a hand between her breasts, pushing the cups of her bra up and making her breasts nearly fall out. Perceptive, he found the latch on the front side of her bra and opened it. She slipped the bra off slowly, and let it fall behind her.

Marissa covered herself with her hands, giving him a little tease. She uncovered first one nipple, then the other. Then she squeezed her arms together, pressing her boobs out for him to enjoy. Ethan gently grabbed her with his fingers, squeezing, then squeezed the other more roughly. He pinched the nipple, rolling it between his fingers.

She scratched his chest while he did that, playing with his nipples too. They exchanged nipple twists, lightly pinching and scratching each other.

And then Marissa reached between her legs, slipping a finger into her pussy to make sure she was wet, and then reached a little further back for his cock. She gave him a not so gentle one handed stroking. She held his hard cock upright and then sat on top of it. He was so big, Marissa didn't know if she could take him all in.

Ethan rubbed her clit, slow and easy. Marissa rotated her hips, enjoying the sensation of his finger and the tip of his cock just inside her. But she wanted more. Very slowly, she sat down further on him. A half inch, then a little more clit stimulation. He massaged her hips and thighs and stomach.

"Good girl," he said.

For him, she slid another half inch. And another. He stretched her out. She loved the feeling of having him inside her, even if he was not even half way in yet.

Marissa lost track of time. Countless times she slid him in

and out, going only a little ways down his shaft. Ethan whispered encouragement to her, telling her how good she was, how hot she made him feel. She worked herself into a hot frenzy. The sticky night air clung to her sweaty skin. Breathing became impossibly hard.

As her pussy dripped and soaked on his cock, she stretched herself even more on him, taking him in almost all the way.

He filled her with his cock. In the moment of passion, he felt right, like his member were made for her body.

Marissa let out all her breath, and slid him in all the fucking way. Balls deep.

"Oh my fucking God baby," she said.

"You okay?" Ethan said.

"Fuck fuck fuck yeah Jesus!" she screamed, bouncing lightly on top of him.

In the very back corner of her brain, she realized somebody might hear her. And in the same corner, she also realized she didn't care what that somebody might think. Marissa almost wanted that to happen. What a show she'd be giving some lucky fool!

So she screamed even louder.

Ethan blushed. Whether from the rush of being screwed, or from embarrassment, Marissa had no idea. She was on a high she'd only experienced a handful of times in her sexual life. She pumped him harder. Skin slapped on skin, echoing off the hedges and the building.

Her pussy clenched him and spat him out in a gushing orgasm. Marissa rubbed her clit rapidly, making more squirt come out. On a roll, she slid his cock back inside and rode him again even harder.

And then she pivoted on his pole and rode him reverse cowgirl style. Ethan clung to her hips, slowly her down some, forcing her to be more gentle. But the way his cock touched and rubbed her G-spot sent her to the moon.

Three more rapid fire, screaming and messy orgasms later, she collapsed into his arms. His body was soaked with her fluids.

He lifted her up and set her down on the bench. Then he ripped off the condom. He stroked himself until he came all over her breasts and face.

Exhausted, Marissa wiped it up with her fingers, smearing it across her skin.

And then Ethan relaxed on top of her, in her arms.

"Holy shit," he said.

"Yes," she said. Marissa couldn't think of anything else to add to that.

She'd think of a better way to thank him later. For now, she gloried in the sensations that were still going on in her pussy. It was like his cock were still inside her.

For a night she had dreaded earlier, this turned out to be one of the best date nights she'd ever been on.

ABOUT THE AUTHOR

Once upon a time, Miriam F. Martin was a princess who ruled a planet Earthlings call Mars. Her reign ended when somebody decided women were really from Venus. Confused about her identity, she ended up between worlds. Putting away her tiara and scepter forever, she now flattens her ass in a cushy chair while writing smutty erotica. You're welcome.

Miriam F. Martin is a pseudonym created by D. Anthony Brown. He owns Hermit Muse Publishing and writes fiction in other genres, including science fiction and fantasy. He lives in Minnesota. His blog is at danthonybrown.com.

Find free erotic fiction and other news about Miriam's stories at SirensGarterErotica.com.

Miriam loves to hear from her fans, and she may be contacted through her agent, David Anthony Brown.

david@danthonybrown.com